ABBY MARTIN: A typical *Aries,* Abby brings the Zodiac Club together. She's always prepared to help others, but her headstrong Aries nature sometimes gets in her way. Will her wild and wonderful whims prevail?

MARA BENNETT: Feminine and charming, she personifies the *Libra* spirit. She appreciates harmony, but it is difficult for her to make a decision. How can she become more decisive?

J.L. RICHTER: Makes cool *Scorpio* a reality with her aloof and independent spirit. Like all Scorpios, she's sure of what she wants and determined to get it. But what is the cost?

ELIZABETH LEONARD: A true *Pisces,* she's a friend who's easily trusted, but her trust in others leaves her vulnerable to being hurt. She has dreams of her own and for every friend in the club. But who comes first?

CATHY ROSEN: Makes her *Leo* sign ring true with confidence and charisma, but her eagerness for praise often overshadows her accomplishments!

JESSICA HOLLY: The friendly, outgoing *Virgo* dreams of finding the right boy and wonders if she'll find a Prince Charming who will meet her expectations. Will her yearnings ever be fulfilled?

PENNY ROSS: A whiz at tennis, she's the perfect *Sagittarius*—zany but endearing! With her flare on the court and her fierce loyalty to her friends she's just not made for the ordinary, but will she make a superstar?

J.L. Richter

Mara Bennett

Elizabeth Leonard

Abby Martin

Jessica Holly

Cathy Rosen

Penny Ross

TAURUS TROUBLE

Including zodiac work profiles

Lynn J. Nichols

Pacer BOOKS FOR YOUNG ADULTS

a member of The Putnam Publishing Group
NEW YORK

Published by Pacer Books,
a member of The Putnam Publishing Group
51 Madison Avenue
New York, New York 10010

RL: 5.9
Pacer is a trademark of The Putnam Publishing Group.
The Zodiac Club is a trademark of The Putnam Pub-
lishing Group.

Printed in the United States of America
First Printing

TAURUS TROUBLE

TAURUS *(April 21–May 21)*

RULING PLANET: *Venus*   **SYMBOL:** *The Bull*

★ ───────────────────────────────

    The Taurus girl needs a sensitive guy, unafraid of emotions. Someone who is neither aggressive nor loud is best able to reach into your heart—without running up against your stubborn nature. Taureans love fun as much as anyone, but also have a deep need for peace and quiet. You thrive on love and are highly romantic. Don't let small problems build up over time; try to discuss them at once. Find boyfriends and girlfriends who can compromise easily. Steady Taurus always comes through for their friends.

★ ───────────────────────────────

RELATIONSHIPS:

Taurus & Aries—better for a friendship than any romance

Taurus & Taurus—a good chance for friendship or romance

Taurus & Gemini—an attraction of opposites, not good for romance

Taurus & Cancer—mutual concerns, humor, goodwill

Taurus & Leo—strong emotions, but often stormy

Taurus & Virgo—an excellent match, with comfort and understanding

Taurus & Libra—attraction, but not enough mutual energy

Taurus & Scorpio—each needs the other

Taurus & Sagittarius—much humor, but very different ideals

Taurus & Capricorn—possible steady, lasting romance

Taurus & Aquarius—better for light friendship

Taurus & Pisces—sweet security and gentle times

"How does it feel to be a winner?" Abby Martin held an imaginary microphone. "Give us a quote, inspire us."

Cathy Rosen ran her hands through her thick black hair as a smile grew across her face. "It's just sinking in. I really have a job on a newspaper."

Abby laughed and shook Cathy's hand. "You beat out fifty kids, you know—pretty stiff competition."

"I'm not afraid of competition." Cathy tossed her head.

"Sure, 'cause you always win," Abby teased proudly.

They made their way through the crowd of kids who were spilling out of the journalism class into the halls, which were already packed. Abby grabbed onto Cathy's arm as Jessica Holly bumped into them from behind.

"Is this a traffic jam or a Zodiac Club meeting?" Jessica complained.

"Shake Cathy's hand," Abby commanded.

"Why—is she Homecoming Queen? Tell me."

Cathy flashed a smile. "You won't believe it, Jess."

"Yes I will." Jessica's pretty mouth pouted as she looked at Cathy. For years, Jessica had envied Cathy's dark curly hair—Jessica had never really liked her own carrot top. She envied Cathy's high marks—Jessica's grades were strictly average. Cathy had a loyal boyfriend—Jessica had chased more boys than Cathy knew but never caught one for long.

"I believe it," she said. "Cathy has all the luck. What is it this time?"

"Come outside where we can talk."

The three girls burst out of the double glass doors of

Collingwood Senior High School, heading for their meeting place under the maple trees on the side lawn.

"Smell that air! I love autumn," Abby exclaimed, throwing her arms wide as if to embrace the air all around them. "And we're finally juniors—genuine upperclassmen. Isn't it great—we have some status around here now."

"It's super—especially now that I'm an intern on the Collingwood *Chronicle*." Cathy brushed at imaginary lint on her thick sweater.

Jessica stared for a minute, then leapt at Cathy, nearly knocking them both over.

"I don't believe it," she cried, hugging her friend fiercely. "No one got it last year! What an honor. You must be good."

"I knew she could do it," Abby said. "Cathy's the best reporter I know."

"The *Chronicle* only takes the best." Jessica's green eyes blinked. "Aren't their editorials always winning awards? I didn't think Cathy was that good!"

"I'd better be," Cathy said, "if I want to impress them. I'm aiming at becoming a stringer."

"What?"

"Stringer—it's a free-lance reporter. They send someone out to cover a story if all the staff reporters are busy."

"You mean you'd get stories printed with your name under them?" Jessica groaned.

"What's wrong, Jess?" Abby asked.

"An ace reporter like Lois Lane! I can't compete with that. I'll never get into the same college as Cathy now."

"Jess, face it—you'll go to any college that has boys." Abby smiled indulgently at Jessica.

"Is it hard to get a story in print with a byline?"

Cathy nodded, her eyes squinted in a familiar determined expression. "Are you kidding? But I'm going to do it. Of course, there are also two Collingwood Academy kids there,

Danny Burns and Jennifer Chow. I wonder what they're like; I bet they're good."

"So what. You're good too." Abby's confidence was unshaken.

"No one from Collingwood ever beat an Academy kid," Jessica worried. "They got all the city club awards last year. They get everything."

"This is a job, not a contest," Abby pointed out.

"Everything is a contest," Jessica said.

"Jess may be right this time." Cathy tried to imagine the two Academy interns but couldn't picture them. "Anyway, I can't worry about it. I've always tried my best before, and I will now."

"How?" Jessica asked scornfully.

"Hey, Jess—those Academy kids won't know what hit them. This is one tough Collingwood junior."

"Maybe you should just enjoy it," Abby said. "Have fun."

Jessica snorted. "Some fun. Working with a couple of snobs."

"Don't jump to conclusions about people," Abby warned her. "We all learned that lesson this summer, remember?"

"You mean ending the rivalry with J.L. Richter and the Hill kids," Cathy said. "You're right. We can't assume the Academy kids are snobs."

"I'd prepare for the worst if I were you," Jessica advised. She gathered her books together quickly. "I've got to run. Jane Timmons has a study date with Ricky Crawford at the library. I thought I'd just happen to be there. Did you see how tall Ricky got this summer? And those muscles! I could die."

She was off and running with a wave of her hand.

Abby laughed. "Poor Jess. Always thinking the worst."

Cathy settled down on the grass. "How should I get them to notice me at the paper?"

"I don't believe it." Sitting down next to Cathy, Abby

rummaged through her pocketbook. "No Leo has trouble drawing attention to herself." She flipped through the well-worn pages of her zodiac book. "'The Leo Woman on the Job,'" she announced, skimming the section for highlights to read out loud. "'It's impossible to ignore the Leo employee,'" she read. "'Leo likes to be in charge, and won't hide his/her light under a bushel. Pay attention to the lion—or else. Lions don't have claws for nothing.'"

Abby glanced up. "Should I keep reading?"

Cathy made a face. "It makes me sound vicious."

"It makes you sound aggressive. And ambitious. And you're sincerely interested in doing a good job."

"I can live with that," Cathy mused. "Anyway, the correct word is 'assertive.' 'Assertive' is confident and direct. 'Aggressive' is a little too pushy for me."

"You need lots of attention. You're ambitious and no one finds that offensive. Be happy—you've got the 'energy of the sun.'"

Cathy had to laugh. "Fire signs are like that."

Elizabeth Leonard and Jim Newman strolled nearby, and Abby excitedly called them over to tell them Cathy's news.

"I'll toast you," Elizabeth cried. "Tabs for everyone at the diner! Or would you rather have champagne at our next Zodiac meeting?"

"Tab now, bubbles later." Cathy grinned.

"You're not greedy," Elizabeth teased.

"I go for all the gusto," Cathy shot back. "Have you seen Will? I haven't told him my big news yet."

"I saw him at the end of last period," Jim answered. "He was driving to the mall—to the computer store, I think."

"Will and his computers!" Cathy sighed. "He won't be back today. Let's go ahead without him."

"I'll drive," Jim offered. "If we can fit in with these art supplies."

Jim led the way around to the parking lot. He and

Elizabeth dumped the heavy boxes they were carrying into the trunk while Cathy and Abby climbed into the backseat of the dusty station wagon.

"Don't lean on your door, Cathy," Jim warned. "The lock's busted. I tied it together with rope."

Cathy shifted her weight toward Abby. "Isn't that a little dangerous?"

Elizabeth leaned over the front seat. "He'll fix it soon. Jim is totally reliable, once he decides to do something. Cancers are like that."

Abby nudged Cathy and whispered, "This is Elizabeth? The one we grew up with? Efficient Elizabeth who always got things done promptly?"

In the front seat Elizabeth and Jim exchanged a look and chuckled. "She's still efficient," he whispered back, making Abby blush in embarrassment.

"Sorry. Didn't mean to let you hear that."

"Leave them alone," Cathy said. "They've got super-powers, now that they're in love."

Elizabeth laughed. "Jim is affecting me. Cancers are pretty easygoing—it's rubbing off."

"Pisces are water signs," Cathy said. "Easily led astray . . . you know, they go with the flow."

"No more horoscope talk," Jim groaned. "Elizabeth drives me crazy with that stuff. I already know exactly how and why we get along. It takes the romance out of things."

"It takes the guesswork out," Elizabeth corrected. "I wouldn't make a fool of myself over someone totally wrong for me. Not after last summer," she added. "If our horoscopes didn't match, I wouldn't be sitting here right now."

"In that case, I love horoscopes and I'll shut up."

Jim grinned and pulled out of the parking lot.

They reached the diner just as a space opened up. Jim pulled in and parked. "All out," he announced.

"Thank you," Cathy exclaimed.

"Your majesty, at your service." Abby swept the door open and bowed low as Cathy climbed as gracefully as possible out of the car, her books spilling from her arms.

"I like these casual ceremonies," Cathy said, bending to pick her French textbook out of the street.

"Me too," Abby agreed.

"I can't wait." Cathy grinned. "The year is starting off so well."

Cathy squinted at the computer screen in front of her. Updating her horoscope program was a lot of work. She wished someone had already done a program that gave each sign's characteristics and detailed with whom they were compatible. Cathy was dying to know what kind of working woman she would be. Finally she turned off the computer and grabbed her book. As a Leo, she knew she was ambitious and determined to win the appreciation of others. But should she step on people's toes on her way up? Should she tone down her aggressive streak and try to fit in? After all, she wasn't going to be a star at the *Chronicle,* only a student intern. It might be worse to be a show-off.

"I want to know everything about journalism," Cathy muttered out loud. "If I blow my first chance, I might not get another one for a long, long time."

She glanced down at her book again. "The Lion shines under the spotlight of responsibility," she read. "Leos may be playful or lazy in their youth, but in maturity they surprise others by their steadfast courage and their ability to carry on despite setbacks or injuries to their overwhelming sense of pride."

"I hope no one hurts my pride on this job," Cathy told the computer. "I'm not sure how noble I can really be."

Cathy closed her eyes and pictured herself in a huge,

bustling newsroom. She was standing before her editor—
an enormous fierce-looking man.

"You call this a story?" he barked at her. "A five-year-
old could write better."

Cathy saw herself kneel on the cold newsroom floor. "I'm
sorry," she sobbed, "I did my best. I asked all my sources
the five questions—who, what, where, when, and how. I
really tried."

"Trying isn't good enough. You're fired."

"I won't take this lying down," Cathy shouted.

The ringing doorbell and the sound of Will Coffman's
voice snapped her out of her daydream. He let himself in
the front door. Tall and dark-eyed, Will was handsome
when he took off his glasses and relaxed. Will was always
being teased about his neat and clean-cut looks. He and
Cathy had known each other forever and everyone assumed
they were a permanent couple—despite their somewhat off-
and-on romance.

"What's with you?" Will threw his jacket onto the couch
and folded his hands across his chest. "Is someone here?"

"No one. Why?"

"Weren't you arguing with someone?"

"No." Cathy quickly put a smile on her face. "I was
thinking out loud."

"Should I come back when your neurotic stage is over?"

"Don't leave. I have news to tell."

"I have some pretty big news to tell you," Will answered,
his eyes twinkling.

"I got a job," Cathy declared proudly.

"I got a job," Will said simultaneously.

"How could you have the same news as me? I wanted to
surprise you."

"I am surprised," Will answered.

"Tell me about your job," Cathy demanded.

Will cleared his throat, sat forward, and said, "Ladies first."

"You rat. Okay, I'll go first. My news is that I'm the one and only Collingwood student who made it as an intern on the *Chronicle*. Isn't that great?"

"It is great." Will leaned over and kissed Cathy noisily on the top of her head.

"What's that?"

"I just had an uncontrollable urge to kiss hair." Will crossed his legs, pushed his wire-rimmed glasses up his nose with one long finger, and grinned at her. "Go on—tell me more. Fill me in on all the gruesome details."

"I don't know many details. I start next week and I'll get assignments from the editor in charge of the intern program."

"Very nice. Almost as good as my new job."

"What? I suppose you want praise for waiting your turn so patiently."

"Ask not what your job can do for you," Will began, grinning at her mysteriously. "Ask what your job can do for your girlfriend."

"Will Coffman, will you tell me already?"

"Then you admit you're my girlfriend?" Will faked an expression of enormous surprise. He fell off his chair and knelt down, hands clasped in front of him. "Thank you, Miss Cathy. Thank you."

"I won't be your girlfriend for long. I won't be speaking to you in a minute."

"That's the Taurus in me." Will grinned. "Taurus teases Leo. You told me so yourself. Doomed to trade insults forever."

"You want insults?" Cathy's voice rose dangerously.

"You're beautiful when you're annoyed. Quick, let's look

up your horoscope and see if Leos are ticklish when they're annoyed."

Will suddenly lunged at her and began jabbing his fingers into her waist.

Cathy couldn't stop laughing. She tried to push him away. "Are you crazy? Stop it." Bent over from the waist and giggling helplessly, she tried to make it to the door, but Will held her back.

"Say you adore me and I'll stop. Go on, 'I adore you more than anyone—even myself. I'm mad for you, Will.' Say it."

"Cathy—better get ready for dinner," Mrs. Rosen's voice called from the kitchen.

"Are you going to leave without telling me?" Cathy asked almost crossly.

"Here's my news. I got a job at the new computer store at the mall—Computer Capers. I'll be working there two nights a week and Saturdays."

"Great," Cathy said, ready to hug him with congratulations.

"That's not all. They have a brand-new program down there."

"What program?"

"It's called Starscope. It's a horoscope program with birthdays and personality traits. It'll save you lots of work."

"Will, that's fantastic!" Cathy hugged him and gave him her most dazzling smile. "Why didn't you just tell me right away?"

"I'm no fool. You won't say you adore me for nothing," Will laughed.

"Maybe I would if you'd give me a chance," Cathy retorted. "If you'd stop teasing all the time, I might want to say it."

"Cathy—dinner!" her mother called again.

"I better leave." Will scooped his jacket off the couch and backed toward the door. "But the girl who loves me most gets first crack at the Starscope program."

"When can I come look at it?"

"When I get a great big kiss."

"That's not likely," Cathy said haughtily. "It's not in your horoscope."

"I know," Will groaned. "I looked it up. 'Underneath all those insults, however, lies a relationship just waiting to take off.'"

Cathy ignored his remark. "When can I come to the store?"

"Saturday should be good. Just be ready to take off."

Will ducked out of the door just in time to escape the pillow Cathy threw at his head.

"Cathy! Are you coming?" her mother called.

"I'm coming. Just hold on."

_____ 2 ★

The mall parking lot was more crowded than usual. Cathy and Jessica climbed out of Jim's car. Elizabeth leaned out the window.

"We'll park and meet you at the computer store."

"Come on, Jess." Cathy slammed the car door. "If they get bored waiting for an empty space, I'm sure they'll think of some way to pass the time."

Cathy and Jessica hurried together into the mall. At least half the teenage population of Collingwood was milling around.

"Same old crowd," Jessica sighed, dismissing the boys huddled together around the newest games at the video arcade. "Isn't there one red-blooded male left who likes girls better than machines? This town needs new blood," she complained. "Or at least a transfusion."

Cathy pulled her along until they came to the Computer Capers store. All the latest in personal computers were on display. It was as quiet as a study hall inside; people sat in front of computer keyboards with salespeople explaining the equipment.

"Not too lively, is it?" Cathy glanced around quickly. "I don't see Will, and I don't want to hang out here. I don't want to ask for him either. We could get him into trouble, since we're not customers."

"There he is." Jessica pointed and Cathy saw Will sitting down behind a computer console near the back of the showroom. A thin, balding man with a wiry beard sat at the keyboard.

"We'd better wait until he's through," Cathy said. But as Will looked up and saw them, he motioned them over.

Jessica led the way toward the back. "Where's my Starscope printout, Coffman?" she asked with a smile, ignoring the bearded man. "Or haven't you had time to goof off on the job yet!"

She elbowed Will lightly and parked a hip on the edge of the console table. The bearded man looked at her.

Cathy gritted her teeth. "Cut it out, Jess. Will is obviously busy. And please keep your voice down."

"It's so empty here, who's going to hear us?" She glanced at the man. "Unless this nice man is Will's boss," she joked.

"Don't I look like a boss?" The small man blinked. His voice was friendly but his face seemed sad. "I *am* his boss, you know." He looked at Jessica with a somber expression.

"This is Harlan Skoglund," Will explained. "He owns

Computer Capers. He is definitely not a typical boss."

Harlan smiled at Will's remark. "That's right. You must be Will's friends. The ones hung up on the zodiac. He's mentioned you to me."

"Right," Cathy said hastily. "We're not hung up on it. We simply have a serious approach to astrology."

"No we don't." Jessica ignored Cathy's dirty look. "We have fun with it all. Especially the good parts—romance and stuff."

"Jessica didn't mean what she said about Will goofing off," Cathy added. "She was just kidding."

"No problem," Harlan answered. "I don't want to alienate teenagers. They're the ones really into computers. It's the parents I have trouble with—convincing them to invest in the things they don't understand. The kids know already."

"Harlan's great," Will said with a smile. "I told him I wanted to run Starscope for you and he said fine. He's the biggest computer nut I've ever met. I'm going to learn a lot here—this job is great."

Harlan stood and motioned to Will to sit at the keyboard. He was barely taller than Cathy and something about him made Cathy want to tell him everything would be all right.

"The computer revolution is the biggest thing to hit this country in decades," he said. "It's changing everything about our lives. Growing up with computers is a fantastic opportunity. You kids are the world of tomorrow. When I was younger, I loved computers, but the people I knew just thought I was a weirdo. Ha-ha. Look at me now!"

"Gee." Jessica blinked at Cathy. "I just wanted to find out which boys were right for me."

"Do you have a computer at home?" Harlan pointed at Cathy.

"Yes."

"And you, Red?" he said to Jessica.

"No." Jessica shook her head. "I don't really need one."

"Wouldn't a word processor make your life easier? How about homework — you could write term papers in no time. How are you at math?"

"Not great," Jessica admitted. "Could a computer do logarithms for me?"

"What you want is what you get. I can make a program for your every need." Harlan tugged at his beard.

"We finally made it!" Elizabeth and Jim crowded up to the computer behind Cathy and Jessica.

Will introduced Harlan and raved about his computer expertise.

"Sounds too good to be true," Jim muttered.

"Sounds wonderful," Elizabeth said.

"It's not too busy here yet, unfortunately. Let's try a printout of Starscope," Harlan suggested. "We still have to work out a few bugs," he explained. He pointed at Cathy. "What's your sign?"

"Leo."

Will typed in several commands.

"Boyfriend's sign?"

Cathy hesitated.

"Will's a Taurus," Jessica answered. "Are you going to run his horoscope too?"

"Compatibility," Harlan said. "We're going to see if Cathy and Will are fated to be together."

"Not a good idea." Cathy put her hand over Will's on the keyboard. "Please don't," she said. "It, uh, it takes all the mystery out."

"What Cathy means," Will stated, "is she doesn't want to see our differences. She thinks it might change things between us. As if we don't already know if we get along or not."

"Makes sense. Why push your luck? Expect trouble and you get it." Jim looked at Elizabeth. "I don't like machines telling people about each other." He rested a hand on Elizabeth's shoulder. "I'm not crazy about this horoscope business, but since Elizabeth tells me we're compatible, I don't make a fuss about it."

Will looked down at the keyboard, but didn't say anything. Jim continued on the subject of horoscopes.

"No two people know if they're right for each other. They have to get together and try to work things out. It's not math—things don't always add up. Facts are facts—not people. That's why I like mechanical things. There are only two ways they work—the right way and the wrong way. A computer isn't meant for stupid guessing games. Am I right, Will?"

Will took off his glasses, polished them on his shirt, and cleared his throat. "If the girls like horoscopes, there's no harm in computerizing them."

"It's ridiculous!" Jim said. "And I know you feel the same way I do, Coffman. Come on, Elizabeth, let's go check out the record store. See you guys later."

"I love horoscopes," Elizabeth called loyally over her shoulder. "Computerized or not."

Cathy walked over to a counter and pretended to study the software, while Harlan and Will, urged on by Jessica, started to print out the Starscope charts. It was a boring process, so Jessica joined Cathy.

"Jim is definitely antizodiac. I expected Will to jump in and blast us too, but he didn't," Jessica said.

Cathy was thoughtful. "Ever since I printed those compatibility charts for my Sweet Sixteen last summer, Will's been really touchy about zodiac stuff. Especially since we weren't tops in the romance department. But he knows the Zodiac Club means a lot to me, so I guess he just wants to be nice. Too bad Jim had to put him on the spot."

Jessica was quiet for a moment. "I don't think you give Will enough credit, Cathy. You're lucky—you have a devoted guy, but you don't appreciate him. You should lay off for a while."

"I'll be easy on him when he's easy on me." Cathy stepped back, offended. "We can't be Mr. and Ms. Perfect Couple. But don't get any ideas about going after Will yourself."

"Would I do that?" Jessica looked insulted.

"Sometimes, Jessica, I'm not sure what you'd do," Cathy said. "Let's go find Jim and Elizabeth."

Twenty minutes later they were all back. Business was still slow.

"Hey, you guys, come get your Starscopes," Will called.

Jessica was the first one there. "It's all about Virgo," she said. "It's wonderful. It includes romance, work, friendship—everything I want to know."

"Jessica went right to the romance part." Elizabeth chuckled.

"Oh no, I'm reading about friendship. I want to see how I fit into the Zodiac Club."

"I want to see how I'm going to handle my junior year," Elizabeth said, sifting through the pile of papers. "There's a lot of pressure with SAT's and achievements to take this year."

As everyone got a chart and began reading out loud to each other, they attracted attention from browsers in the store. Many people were interested in horoscope printouts for themselves. Harlan became busy trying to meet all the requests for printouts.

"Will," he whispered, "put Starscope away before I become a free horoscope service."

"I can't believe all these people are so excited about their horoscopes," Jessica exclaimed. "They're adults."

"Everyone knows his sign," Harlan said. "It's something people can't seem to resist."

"You should be in the horoscope business," Jessica joked. "It's a phenomenon."

A light seemed to go on in Cathy's eyes. Will had seen that look before. "Watch out—Cathy has an idea," he warned.

"Why not use horoscopes to promote the store?" Cathy turned to Harlan. "You could advertise a free Starscope chart for every customer. You'd get a lot of people in—and even if they don't buy a computer, they might end up buying the Starscope disk.

"It's not a bad idea." Harlan pulled at his wiry beard. "But free horoscopes for everyone would be impossible. I'd get every kid in Collingwood in here. I'd lose money and scare away serious customers."

"You could limit it some way," Elizabeth suggested. "Maybe charge a small fee."

"I've got a better idea." Cathy's voice rose in excitement. "Each month you feature one horoscope, and give birthday-present suggestions for that month's sign. You know, according to age, sex, hobbies. All the stores in the mall would profit. Maybe they'd split the costs with you."

"And during the holidays you could print all the signs. For people buying presents. But it shouldn't be free," Will said, "or paid for by the stores. You could get more publicity out of it if you sold the horoscopes for a dollar, got the other stores to chip in a few cents for each dollar earned, and donated the profits to some local charity."

"That's it. That's perfect," Cathy cried. "You get publicity for your store and you help a charity too."

"That appeals to me," Harlan said. "But..."

"It's a great publicity scheme," Cathy protested.

"The idea sounds good," Harlan agreed. "But there's a tremendous amount of work involved. I'd have to hire people to print all those charts. It isn't something a new business like mine can afford."

"Maybe the Zodiac Club can help you," Jessica said.

"What could you do?" Harlan asked.

"So far all we've done is hold meetings—no boys in sight," Jess complained.

"We've had fun, Jess," said Elizabeth. "But maybe this is our chance to get involved in some useful projects. We could help your store get on its feet and make money for charity."

"That's right," Cathy agreed. "Nursing homes, or after-school projects, things like that. We could check around and determine what worthy cause to help. What do you say, Mr. Skoglund?" Cathy held out a hand eagerly. "Of course, the Zodiacs will have to vote on the idea—but why not let us work for you. We'll run the programs and help bring the people in."

"Call me Harlan." He grinned. "If we're going to work together, let's keep it friendly. You discuss it with your members and let me know. Your parents will have to agree. I'm not so sure the other stores will go along with us, but I'm willing to try for a few weeks."

"Fabulous!" Cathy said.

Harlan smiled slowly. "Business could be better," he finally said. "And it might be for a worthy cause."

"Absolutely. As soon as we figure out which charity, we'll let you know." Cathy smiled, then looked at all her friends. "We found a way to make ourselves useful. That's what Zodiacs should be all about."

They all shook hands with Harlan and said good-bye to Will. They found the car in the farthest reaches of the lot and headed home. Cathy sat pondering the Starscope chart as she pulled it eagerly from her pocketbook. She read silently for a while, then whistled softly.

Jessica turned to look at her. "What?"

"You were right, Jessica. I hate to admit it—but I don't give Will enough credit. Look at this chart. He had it fixed so Leo and Taurus come out as a perfect match—in friendship and romance." She shook her head in wonder. "What do you do with a guy like that?"

Jessica pursed her lips. "If you don't know, I'm not going to tell you."

_____ 3 ★

It was thrilling to get out of school early—especially to go to work. Cathy shoved a few leaves around with her foot and watched anxiously for her mother's car. She tried to hide her anger at not being able to get the car herself on her first day at the *Chronicle*. Hopefully no one would see her mother drop her off. Her younger sister Jane had to be taken to the doctor that afternoon, so Cathy was stuck. And anything was better than taking the bus.

Finally her mother's silver Honda pulled up to the curb. Cathy ran down the steps, piled into the front seat, and planted a quick kiss on her mother's cheek.

"Cath—good luck at the paper," Jane said from behind.

"What did you borrow, Jane?"

Her mother shook her head.

"You know, Mother, Jane never says anything nice to me on purpose."

"If you thought about it, you'd realize Jane admires you, Cathy," her mother replied.

"Could have fooled me." But Cathy was pleased and swiveled to look at her sister.

"Jane—stop that," Mrs. Rosen ordered. "If you're going

to spend all that time over your hair, at least don't make it worse."

Jane's hand dropped automatically. "I'm just twisting it to make it curl," she protested.

Jane had beautiful, shiny honey-colored hair, their father's color. Naturally, she constantly wished for glossy dark curls like Cathy's. Jane was also envious that Cathy had gotten the blue eyes in the family.

"What I wanted to say was do well on your first day." Jane's voice was cranky again—as usual. "Who knows what will happen on your second."

"Dear old Jane." Cathy grinned. "Typical twelve-year-old."

"Don't say that. You should be nicer to me, shouldn't she, Mom? You should take me places with you and invite me to all your parties. I didn't even get invited to that Sweet Sixteen party your friends gave you."

"You're never going to forget that, are you?"

"Why should I?"

"Because you were away at camp and didn't want to come home for the party, if you remember correctly."

"You should have waited."

Cathy laughed. "Jane, someday I'll make it up to you. I promise."

Her mother pulled up in front of the *Chronicle*'s offices. A large plate-glass window was filled with pictures of people and places in the community. Cathy had been to the office once before, to place a classified ad when her father had sold their old car. Now all her self-confidence drained away.

"Call if you need a ride home," her mother said before pulling away.

Cathy swallowed and walked inside to a long counter across the reception area. Behind it, a woman was answering the telephone. She looked up, motioning to Cathy to wait while she finished her call.

"Finally," she said, putting the receiver down. "May I help you?"

Cathy introduced herself as a new intern on the work-study program.

"You need to see Mrs. Mead, the editor. She'll be expecting you. The other two are already here. I'm Helen Cavanaugh, receptionist and grandmother."

The woman's eyes were warm and friendly, much younger than the eyes of any ordinary grandmother.

"You don't look like a grandmother," Cathy blurted out, but Helen looked pleased so Cathy realized it was the right thing to say.

"Would you believe this mother of five, grandmother of two was once a model?"

"Yes I would," Cathy answered. She could see that underneath the lined face there might once have been a beautiful woman with high cheekbones and big eyes.

"Good girl." Helen winked at her. "You'll make a terrific reporter. Now I'll point out Mrs. Mead's office while you're still on time."

Cathy hurried across the newsroom, a smaller version of the big impressive newsrooms she had seen on television shows. It wasn't very glamorous-looking—mostly it looked like one big office.

Cathy found Mrs. Mead's door, knocked, and entered. Inside, the girl and boy from Collingwood Academy glanced up at her, and Cathy smiled automatically in greeting. She noticed they didn't smile back. Then Mrs. Mead spoke.

"You're Cathy Rosen." It sounded like a command, not a greeting. Cathy nodded, caught off guard by Mrs. Mead's steely voice and no-nonsense manner.

"Have a seat. Your fellow interns—Danny Burns, Jennifer Chow." Cathy nodded at each in turn, just long enough to register that they weren't really interested in her at all.

Both were focusing on Mrs. Mead. Cathy took her seat, studying her new boss. Mrs. Mead looked more of the grandmother type than Helen had. She was round all over and sported old-fashioned glasses on a chain around her neck. Even her gray hair, cut short and straight with little bangs, lent her an air of coziness. The contrast between looks and personality couldn't have been sharper.

"We don't waste anything at the *Chronicle*," Mrs. Mead stated like an army sergeant. "Not time, not money, not effort by any of our employees." No one said a word.

"We're small, but we're one of the best weeklies in the Northeast. You can help us. As interns you'll get an overview of the editorial process—but there's a lot more to a newspaper than writing columns and articles. So forget your notions of the glamour of this business, here and now."

Cathy raised her eyebrows, sneaking a look at Danny and Jennifer. They sat perfectly composed, and it was obvious neither had any idea that newspaper work was glamorous.

"Ads sell papers. Our advertisers buy the space for their ads on each page. Our news is important, but so are the ads. Remember that. Unsold advertising space means fewer pages for articles. Get the concept? Most people don't understand that basic fact of newspaper life."

Cathy nodded—as calm and collected as Danny and Jennifer.

Mrs. Mead flashed a totally unexpected smile and was suddenly as kind as Cathy had suspected she was.

"Now, for your jobs. Everyone starts at the same place—the bottom. You may run errands and fetch copy from place to place. But in order to use your brains, you'll also rewrite, do copy editing and proofreading. You have the honor of keeping the back-issue room neat, of ordering the darkroom and making fresh coffee when needed. But don't despair," she said, "one of you may get something into print. We like our interns to submit ideas for stories, in fact. But let me tell you a little story."

Cathy held her breath, not daring to relax. Mrs. Mead sat on the corner of her desk. She didn't look anything at all like a grandmother now.

She paused to wipe her glasses, chuckling to herself. "We had one girl here—she tried to scoop a columnist on the local teachers' strike story. In her boundless enthusiasm, she got a few of her facts wrong. If we had used her story, we'd have been slapped with a lawsuit. You can imagine her enthusiasm and then ours. You get my point?"

She peered at them over her shiny steel rims, but her smile was kind.

"There aren't many second chances, in my opinion. Do it right the first time—that's my motto."

She got up off her desk. "Now, if I haven't scared you to death, I'll be glad to answer any questions you have. I'm here to teach you as much as possible about newspapers. I love them. If you love them too, we'll get along just fine."

Someone stuck his head in the door. "Hattie, there's a problem. Can you come?"

"Excuse me," Mrs. Mead told them. "I'll be right back."

The small room was quiet after Mrs. Mead left. Cathy realized she had been holding her breath, and she exhaled in one long sigh of relief.

"Welcome to the *Chronicle*," she muttered.

Jennifer looked at her, not saying a word. Cathy instantly regretted her comment. Was Jennifer the type to report her sarcastic remark to Mrs. Mead? she wondered. She decided to keep her mouth shut and act more serious, until Danny Burns piped up. He whistled, long and loud.

"What is she, an editor or a prison warden? I'll bet she eats high-school interns for breakfast."

"No," Cathy added, "I bet she's a mobster boss who usually spends her time hiring hit men."

"Nope," Danny answered drily. "She's a referee at prize-fights."

"She *is* a prizefighter," Cathy declared. "Unchallenged heavyweight champ." She and Danny broke up—but Jennifer still sat quietly, seemingly not even listening to them.

"It's got to ease up after this," Cathy said. "Otherwise we'd never do anything. Can you imagine what she's like when you mess up? I'd hate to be around to see her angry."

"You mean she's in a good mood now?" Danny rolled his eyes comically, glancing at Jennifer. She stared back at him. "What did we get ourselves into?" he said.

The turning doorknob alerted them, and they were all sitting straight and sober when someone new entered the room.

"Mrs. Mead is tied up," he told them.

"Who tied her?" Danny whispered. Cathy almost choked, trying not to laugh.

"I'm Charlie Ahearn," the man said. "I'm an editor here, and I'll give you a quick tour of the building before you get your assignments today. Follow me, please."

As they were crossing the newsroom, Cathy spotted Mrs. Mead talking quietly with two people. To her surprise, Mrs. Mead patted the man on the back and seemed to be comforting him about something. Maybe there was hope after all, Cathy mused. Mrs. Mead might be human.

By the time they had finished their tour, Cathy understood what Mrs. Mead had meant.

"There certainly is more to this than writing stories," she commented to Charlie Ahearn. "Paste-ups and typesetting, proofing copy, selling ads—just like Mrs. Mead said, the articles are not the only thing anyone thinks about."

"But finally the most important of all," he said. He held up a hand as Cathy started to protest. "I know what Mrs. Mead told you. Ads sell papers. But remember this—she cares deeply about the quality of the articles we print. Don't ever think you can slide by with inferior reporting or slip-shod writing. It won't wash. Mrs. Mead knows her stuff. You kids keep your eyes and ears open and you'll learn a lot from her."

"Why hasn't she moved to a bigger newspaper?" Danny asked, brushing his hair off his forehead. "How come she stays with a weekly? Couldn't she make a lot more money on a big city paper?"

Charlie Ahearn put his hands on his hips and looked from one of them to the other. "Everyone has his own private dream," he said finally. "There aren't many small-time newspapers left nowadays. It used to be one of the most vital jobs in any community—editor. Let's just say Mrs. Mead is an old-fashioned romantic. All she wants is to put out a good paper and be respected for it."

He showed them back to the main newsroom and left them at Mrs. Mead's office. "Some of us just love news-papers," he said as he left them.

"Mrs. Mead an old-fashioned romantic?" Danny was skeptical.

Jennifer frowned at Danny. "She only wants us to take the job seriously. Which I do."

"I bet you do. You can't wait for a chance to butter up dear Mrs. Mead. I wouldn't be surprised if you ended up looking just like her someday."

"At least I wouldn't be the class clown," Jennifer said sarcastically.

Jennifer caught Cathy's startled reaction. "Ignore us," she said, clearly embarrassed. "Talk about first impressions!"

"It's okay."

"No, I'm sorry. When I'm nervous, I talk too much."

"Me too," Danny admitted. "Don't give up hope—I'm a nice guy, really."

Mrs. Mead returned and gave them their assignments.

"Burns—go to the darkroom. Jed Priess is there to show you what to do."

Danny's carefree smile faded. "Darkroom? I don't know photography."

"You don't have to, just clean up in there and you'll learn about it." Mrs. Mead wrote something in her notebook. Danny stared at her, then at Jennifer. "I was editor of *Academy Blues* all last year," he began to protest. One glance from Mrs. Mead's gray eyes raised over those glinty frames and Danny's mouth shut firmly. He turned obediently toward the door.

"Rosen and Chow, see Alice Stein, city desk."

Cathy's hopes rose. City desk! When her assignment and Jennifer's turned out to be proofreading columns of typeset copy, her spirits dropped. Boring minutes of the town council meeting and endless local ordinances were read and checked. She was glad she already knew the proofing symbols.

The two girls sat at adjoining desks in a corner of the big newsroom.

"Rosen and Chow," Jennifer said in a deadpan voice as she looked at Cathy. "Sounds like a vaudeville team—comedy and proofreading." She shook her straight black hair and bent over piles of copy, checking for mistakes.

Cathy grinned. "This is boring, but we have to take it seriously."

"Serious people love to be silly," Jennifer confided.

"You and Danny Burns must know each other already."

"Yeah."

"Is he silly? Do you get along?"

"He gets good grades. He's very intelligent," she said primly.

"You know, Jennifer—it would probably be easier if you could make friends with Danny."

Jennifer gaped at her.

"I know it's none of my business," Cathy said hastily. "I'm no expert on boys—you should meet my boyfriend someday. But boys have a hard time talking to smart, pretty girls like you. Maybe Danny's just uncomfortable around you."

Jennifer was watching her closely.

"Why are you telling me this?"

"I'm like that; I'm a Leo, with a big mouth."

"I guess you're trying to be nice," Jennifer said.

"I know I shouldn't butt in."

"Look—thanks for the friendly advice, but I'm not after Danny Burns. And I'm glad you already have a boyfriend. It would be a mistake to be interested in Danny. That's my friendly advice."

"Well, thanks," Cathy said uncertainly.

It wasn't a really great conversation, but at least Jennifer seemed friendlier than she had at first. Cathy was dying to ask her more questions, but Jennifer was deep in the pile of proofreading again. Cathy plunged into her own work.

The time passed quickly and Cathy soon dropped her finished copy at the city editor's desk. Jennifer had gotten up to leave at the same time and Cathy smiled politely as Jennifer moved ahead of her. Jennifer paused at the front door, holding it open for Cathy.

"Thanks."

A city bus was pulling away from the curb as they left the *Chronicle* building.

"Missed it!" Cathy snapped her finger.

Jennifer hesitated. "Where're you going?"

Cathy recited her address. "It's a pain when my mom needs the car," she added.

Jennifer hesitated again. "My car's here," she said, "but I can't take you all the way. I'm going to the library."

"Now? I mean, aren't you going home for dinner first?"

"I'll grab a sandwich. I usually eat again when I get home later."

"You go to the library every day?"

"Of course." Jennifer seemed surprised at the question. "You have to, to get top grades at the Academy."

"Listen, I'll take the next bus, no problem. Don't wreck your schedule for me."

"I have a new routine," Jennifer explained, "because of this internship. I've always kept my afternoons free for studying at the library so I'm clear for review sessions at night."

"Review sessions? You mean, you and your friends get together at night?"

"No—my parents take turns working with me, alternate nights. This job means I have to squeeze my library work in before review sessions."

"You work that hard?"

Jennifer glanced at her watch. "It's not weird—all my friends do it."

Cathy shivered. "I'll take that ride, if you don't mind."

"Sure—it's cold tonight."

Jennifer led Cathy around to the parking lot, where she unlocked a new Toyota.

"Just throw those books in back."

Cathy swept the pile of books off the passenger seat and got in.

"This car's fantastic—stick shift?"

Jennifer nodded, pulling out onto the street. "Yeah, I hate automatics. You don't *do* anything."

Cathy settled back and watched the town whiz by.

"You're a good driver," she remarked.

"Thanks—I love driving. I love to be out alone, radio on—just moving. It's probably the most relaxing part of my schedule."

"Oh."

They drove in silence.

"Drop me here." Cathy got ready to leave the car.

"Cathy...I'm glad we're working together."

"Yeah...it'll be good."

Cathy slammed the door and waved good-bye.

Sitting in her room after dinner, Cathy reached automatically for her magazine. Her hand wavered and pulled her history text out of a pile of schoolbooks. She found herself reviewing the last two chapters, then reading through the next one. It felt good. Maybe she'd organize a "new schedule." There was no harm in borrowing Jennifer's techniques—if they paid off.

_____ 4 ★

J.L. Richter crumpled her empty paper cup and tossed it expertly into a trash bin.

"So where are they?"

She sat down next to Elizabeth on the edge of one of the indoor planters lining the concourse in the mall.

"Cathy will be here." Abby drained her cup, crumpled it, aimed for the trash bin, and missed. "She and Jessica are coming together and I know they wouldn't miss this meeting."

"She'd better not." J.L. bit down on her last ice cube. "This whole Starscope project was her idea. Look, there's Penny and Mara."

"Great. Everyone's here except Jess and Cathy."

"Strange place for a Zodiac meeting." Mara Bennett shoved J.L. aside and found herself a place on the planter wall.

The others pulled up chairs from the wrought-iron tables outside the Pizza Plaza.

"I'll buy something to drink and a slice," Elizabeth offered. "We can all pick at one piece of pizza. That should buy us time at the tables."

Cathy and Jessica came running up with Cathy's sister Jane not far behind.

"Sorry we're late." Cathy paused for breath. "My mom insisted I take Jane to the mall."

"I got ready as fast as I could." Jane looked around, smiling. She nudged Cathy in the ribs. "Well? Ask them."

"Ask us what?" J.L. glanced suspiciously at Cathy.

"Nothing. Not worth discussing." Cathy glared at Jane.

"Don't make me ask, Cathy. Please," Jane begged.

Cathy growled. "Jane would like to belong to the Zodiacs. I told her no way, but unfortunately my mother thinks that's unfair of me and would like you girls to tell Jane."

Mara and Penny whispered together. "There aren't any sixth-graders in the club, Jane," Mara said kindly.

"And no other little sisters," Cathy pointed out.

"And you wouldn't be able to bring your own friends in," Penny added, "so you'd have to spend all your time with us."

Elizabeth frowned. "We never made up laws about who could join. We were all friends, so we started a club. If we expand, we'll have to get so formal."

"She's right," Abby said. "We all hang out together anyway. I don't think any of us want to be mean, but we aren't really looking for more members."

"But I'm around anyway," Jane protested. "And I already know all of you."

"I don't get it. Why do you want to join suddenly?" Cathy paused for a sip of Elizabeth's drink. "You have plenty of friends your own age."

"You're after something," Jessica accused.

"Oh, forget it," Jane said. "I thought I could meet some cute boys this way—someone older. But if you're going to be mean, it isn't worth it. I'll meet them on my own."

"Boys!" Cathy sputtered. "I thought you wanted to spend more time with me. Now I get it."

"And you can forget it," Jessica said. "Any boys we find, we keep for ourselves. Me first."

"Besides, we didn't form this club to meet boys," J.L. pointed out. "We're dedicated to friendship—first and foremost. And that means girls together."

"Right," said Mara and Penny.

"Absolutely," added Elizabeth and Abby.

Everyone had spoken except Jessica.

"Jess?"

"I have nothing against boys in the club."

"Jessica!" Cathy glared at her.

"Never mind," Jane interrupted. "I'm better off on my own. Who wants to hang out with a bunch of draggy juniors anyway. I'll be back later for a ride home." Jane flounced off to the other end of the mall.

"Old and draggy?" Abby looked dismayed. "At sixteen?"

"Oh, Jane's just a child." Cathy dismissed her. "We have important things to discuss today. We have stores to cover."

"Forget the stores for a minute," Mara said. "How'd it go at the *Chronicle* yesterday? What are the kids from the Academy like?"

"Good—I think." Cathy swallowed a mouthful. "The other girl, Jennifer Chow—she's a workhorse. I barely talked to her. The boy, Danny Burns—he doesn't seem bad at all. He has a sense of humor."

"And cute?" Jessica asked hopefully.

"Depends—if you like them tall with big eyes," Cathy teased. "And it seems Will knows Danny. They were at summer camp together in junior high. Will liked him a lot."

"But what does he look like?" Jessica persisted.

"What's his sign?" Abby said. "That's always interesting to know."

"Believe it or not, that wasn't the first thing I asked. Especially since there was a dragon breathing down my neck. And I mean our editor, Hattie Mead."

"She's bad news, huh?"

"The worst," Cathy groaned. "Strictly no-nonsense. Which is okay by me. I intend to be the best intern there anyway."

"Good. Then you don't want that boy, and I can have him."

"Jessica, maybe you should see what he's like first." Abby stood up and stretched.

"Hold it, Jessica. I've only worked one day. I'm trying to make a good impression."

"We're forgetting we have work to do," J.L. chided them. "Starscope and charity? Remember?"

Cathy glanced at her watch. "We'd better get over to Computer Capers before Will flips out. And Harlan too."

"What do you think of Harlan?" J.L. asked as they hurried through the mall. "I never trust adults who try to be chummy with kids."

"Will says he just likes kids. He's not married. He's okay," Cathy said.

"Where'd he get a weird name like Harlan?" Jessica asked.

"It's not weird. I have a cousin and an uncle named Harlan," J.L. said.

"Then it's a Southern name," Jessica announced. "And Southerners are gentlemen. That's a well-known fact."

"Honestly. We all read *Gone with the Wind*," Penny advised. "So spare us your wisdom."

Harlan and Will were waiting with Starscope charts.

"Let me get this straight," Abby said. "We show them the Starscope charts and explain the idea for a horoscope promotion. The stores contribute toward the costs. In return, they're featured as stores with gifts for every sign of the zodiac."

"Correct. That last bit was Cathy's brainstorm," Will announced. "They shouldn't refuse. After all, it's for a good cause."

"The best," J.L. said. "My mom's on the board of Oak Tree. They have a day-care service. They really need money and they do good work."

"And they can use the money raised to buy computer equipment," Harlan explained.

J.L. beamed. "I knew they were sold the minute my mother called them."

Mara was perplexed. "What will computers be used for?"

"Oak Tree needs computers for organizational purposes and to use as teaching tools," Harlan said.

"I get it," Mara answered.

"Good," Harlan said, "because you can't sell anyone on an idea unless you believe in it yourself."

"That's what my mother says." J.L. grinned in delight. "Great salespeople think alike, I guess."

"Let's meet back here in two hours," Cathy suggested. "I bet we sell every store in the mall on this idea."

Two hours later, the group gathered and their news was far from triumphant.

"The store managers don't think there's enough in it for them," J.L. explained. "It makes me pretty cynical about people, believe me."

"Don't give up," Cathy begged them. Mara and J.L. glared at her. "I know—I had my share of cold shoulders today too. But we can't expect instant results."

"I did," Penny complained. "I thought this would be easy. And it's terrible. I felt like a beggar."

Harlan smiled. "It's too tough. I knew it. Maybe we should drop the whole thing. I hate to see you kids discouraged."

"Hey, selling is tough," Will said. "Believe me, I know, now that I'm a working salesman."

"Will's right," Cathy pleaded. "Half of good salesmanship is persistence. J.L.—you know I'm right."

"I guess."

"Let's give it another try tomorrow, and the day after too," Mara suggested.

"I'm for that," Elizabeth and Abby agreed, and soon everyone was enthusiastic again.

"I'm willing to work, don't get me wrong," Jessica explained. "If we have to do this thing, I'll do it right. Don't worry."

Cathy hugged her. "You have a good heart, Jess."

"For all our faults, Virgos hate to leave a job unfinished," Jessica said. "You can count on me."

"Remind me of this the next time I want to wring her neck," J.L. whispered to Abby.

They arranged to come back to the mall again, working in pairs to sign up more store owners. Cathy felt a pang of anxiety. She was going to have an awfully tight schedule, between school, the *Chronicle,* and Starscope.

"Cathy, you look worried about something," Abby said.

"No—nothing," Cathy said.

Will showed them how to run the Starscope programs. Saturday they could set up a computer table in front of the store.

"We'll work in shifts on the weekend," Abby suggested. "That way no one will get stuck with all the work."

Cathy nodded absently. "Yeah . . . great."

"Okay—we'll sign up more stores during the week, and

Saturday will be Starscope's maiden voyage." Abby had spoken for her, Cathy realized. As the others split up to go home, Abby drew Cathy aside.

"Listen, this was your idea. You're still into it, aren't you?"

"Sure thing. No problem." Cathy smiled. "It might be tight, but I've managed tight schedules before. Nothing could keep me away."

---------------------------------- 5 ★

"It's the Rosen and Chow Show." Jennifer bowed to an imaginary audience, smiling wryly as she and Cathy took seats around a big wooden table. Danny was to join them, having complained about his darkroom assignment the other day.

"I wouldn't complain to Mrs. Mead if I were Danny," Cathy remarked. "That woman seems to like testing us."

"I think it's Mrs. Mead's idea of fun. And I wouldn't want to fail one of her tests. I need college recommendations—I want her on my side."

Danny sat down and Jennifer got right to work.

The pages to be edited lay in the center of the wooden table. Cathy was barely through with her first column of corrections when Danny Burns's hand shot out, taking a fresh sheet of copy from the stack. Cathy frowned and tried reading faster. When Jennifer's hand reached out for a piece of copy, Cathy shifted uncomfortably—she still had a way to go. She quickly glanced over the remaining paragraphs—they seemed fine. Relieved, she grabbed a new piece of copy.

Danny Burns, a feverish look in his eye, put down his blue copy-marking pencil and took the next sheet of paper from the pile.

It was hopeless—no way could Cathy catch up to them. She sat back with her slip of type, working carefully down the rows of words to find transposed letters and misplaced commas. Jennifer's hand reached out for yet more copy.

Maybe this is simpler than I thought. Cathy forced her eyes over the type faster and faster—yet Danny and Jennifer were marking off two sheets of copy to her one. She was caught up in the rhythm of their reaching hands, trying desperately to be accurate and yet finish as quickly as they did.

Danny got up with a pile of copy and brought it to the editor's desk. Cathy allowed herself to collapse, sighing out loud.

"Is he kidding? And you—how fast can you read?"

"What?" Jennifer seemed to have forgotten Cathy was there. She grinned. "Oh, you noticed our little race? It happens all the time. Danny hates me to beat him at anything."

Cathy eyed Jennifer.

"Don't laugh—but what sign are you?"

Jennifer put down her pencil. "Taurus. Why?"

Cathy let out a loud groan. "Not another one!"

"What? Who?" Jennifer looked around as if expecting to see someone behind them. "Another one what?"

"Taurus," Cathy said. "My boyfriend Will is a Taurus— and we have this crazy relationship! We like each other a lot, but we're always ranking one another out. Everyone calls us a good couple, but I don't know. Romance isn't supposed to be a name-calling contest."

Jennifer put down her pencil. "I can relate to that, but I don't know much about horoscopes. I come from a scientific family."

"How's that?"

"My father's a research chemist and my mom's an engineer. They both believe in precision and facts. I was not raised on fairy tales and magic. No one ever told me to believe in Santa Claus or fairy godmothers. I got a complete scientific explanation for anything and everything."

"No tooth fairy?"

"No way."

"I guess you think horoscopes are pretty stupid, then."

"Actually," Jennifer said, looking over her shoulder again, "I think they're lots of fun."

"Fantastic!" Cathy said, smiling. "Only . . . you're not a bit like Will, though you both have a sarcastic streak. I don't know. Maybe the Taurus male is different from the Taurus female."

"I hope so."

"They *must* be different." Cathy grinned. "You couldn't possibly be as fussy and stubborn as Will."

Jennifer's dimple showed. "I can be pretty stubborn." Her smile faded and she looked at Cathy thoughtfully. "There's another Taurus I know. And he's a bit of a problem for me too. Like Will and you."

"Who?" Cathy leaned forward, thrilled to share Jennifer's boy problems.

Jennifer gestured toward the editor's desk, where Danny was scowling over pages of rough copy. He looked up as Cathy and Jennifer watched him, and flashed them a sunny smile.

"Danny Burns?"

"None other."

"I thought you didn't like him. You wouldn't talk or laugh at his jokes the first day."

"I know. Good old D.B. and I have had our share of problems. He was showing off for you. Maybe I was jealous."

"Are you dating? Don't answer if it's too personal," Cathy added.

"No—no dates now. We dated for a while, then it fell apart. I don't know what we are now. Friends, I guess."

"There are other boys."

"No one's as much fun as Danny," Jennifer insisted. "He loves bad jokes, and there's something so sweet about him. Notice how enthusiastic he is? He'll do anything, and he has tons of energy."

She might not admit it, but Jennifer still liked Danny Burns. Any fool could see that.

"One time he organized a whole ice-sculpture contest on the Academy lawn—on the spur of the moment. Fantastic—you wouldn't believe the statues. We even got in the paper. Typical Burns stunt; no one's like that."

Jennifer caught herself and stopped short. "The trouble is, he doesn't discriminate. He goes after everything that way. It's fun—but also a contest. And Danny hates to lose contests."

Jennifer bit her lip and looked away.

"Sometimes," Cathy said slowly, "the same signs have trouble getting along. Maybe you can't do anything about it."

Jennifer nodded mournfully. "Probably not. What about us—how are our signs together?"

"I'll tell you what. I'll look it up tonight. But don't worry, I know I like you."

Jennifer smiled in relief. "That's great."

"I'll call you, okay?"

"Sure."

"Give me your number." Cathy dug through her pocketbook for a pencil. "I bet a Taurus female and a Leo female can be great friends."

Jennifer smiled and they exchanged numbers.

* * *

When Cathy got home she checked her horoscope books and looked up Taurus-Leo friendships. While she was at it, she looked up Taurus-Taurus romance for Jennifer.

When her mother called Cathy to the phone that night, she already knew it was Jennifer, and she had the good news prepared.

"Cathy? I can't talk long. My dad is giving me a physics review tonight. But I had to find out about my sign first."

"Your family *is* serious about your grades. You sure weren't kidding."

"I told you—in my house you're expected to be the best." Jennifer spoke softly. "An assignment comes first with me, always. If I have to, I'll break a date with a friend to get work done. Now you see what I'm really like."

"I don't know what to say. The internship is important to me too."

"But not like that."

"I guess if I had plans with friends, I'd keep them."

"See? You're a nicer person." Jennifer's muffled voice became clear again. "Sorry. My mom wants me off the phone. Listen, don't give up on me. Maybe when I get into my first-choice college I can relax and be normal. But you know how it is when you have a goal. Nothing gets in the way."

"Typical Taurus," Cathy said lightly.

"Well, before I have to go—tell me. How'd I do, according to the stars?"

"I'll give you the highlights. First of all, you and I should have no trouble getting along."

There was a relieved giggle on the other end.

"Actually, Taurus is one of the few signs Leos have serious, long-term friendships with. Except that we're both stubborn and strong-willed, so we have to remember to let the other person have her way once in a while."

"You're stubborn too? Mom's always telling me I'm impossible to deal with."

"She's right. I'm the same way—always wanting to be in the spotlight too. That's a Leo trait."

"You're not conceited, though. You don't brag about yourself."

"Give me something to brag about, and I will," Cathy teased. "I like being a leader. You should hear about the project I dreamed up for my Zodiac Club."

"You have a club about the zodiac?"

"Me and six other girls. I'll tell you about it."

"Not now," Jennifer apologized. "I really have to go."

"Okay—then I'll get to the good stuff." Cathy propped her feet up just as the door opened and Jane made a face at her.

"I'll be right off," Cathy said. Jane grimaced.

"As far as you and Danny go, Taurus-Taurus can be a problem. You click instantly and are attracted to one another—probably because you're so much alike." Cathy raised her eyebrows. "You're both warm, earthy, and sensual."

Jennifer giggled. "No comment."

"Your stubborn streak is the problem. You both need someone who can compromise. You both make up your minds about things before they even happen. But if you're aware of that, you can work it out. You can be a dynamite couple."

"But who wants to spend all the time working at it?" Jennifer sighed. "Do I really want Danny Burns?"

Cathy sat straight up, gesturing although no one could see her. "That's how I feel about Will sometimes. Then I get mad at myself for being lazy and selfish. I don't know what's right—find someone you never have problems with? Or work things out?"

"Search me."

"I really want someone to sweep me off my feet. And

Will would take that literally. He's sweet, but hopeless."

Jane looked angrily at her sister. "If you don't get off, I'll kill you. I'm expecting an important call."

"Excuse me," Cathy said with exaggerated politeness. "Ms. Jane needs the telephone. Children are so tiresome."

"Okay, I've got to go anyway."

"Listen, maybe we could get together Sunday. I'm spending most of Saturday with the Zodiacs at the mall."

"Sunday may not be good. I don't know. I'll call you if I get a chance. 'Bye."

Cathy sat staring at the phone after she hung up. She was thinking about the *Chronicle,* about her own vague dream of working for a big newspaper someday. Jennifer was so focused, so intense. Is that what it took to be a winner? And if it was, could Cathy make it? She had promised herself she'd be the best intern, show up the Academy kids—but maybe they already had her beat. Jennifer seemed to want to win so much more.

"How will you amount to anything if you spend all your time gabbing on the phone?" Jane said, mimicking their mother.

She was only teasing, but Cathy didn't come back with a snappy answer. She sat and thought about Jane's comment. What price was she willing to pay in order to win?

She turned back to her Zodiac book and read about each sign's attitude toward work:

Zodiac work profiles

ARIES: Arians do well in endeavors where design and detail are combined. They enjoy working with the public, yet don't need immediate gratification. Those born under the sign of the Ram do especially well in creative roles.

TAURUS: Taureans are frequently outstanding workers and may exhibit admirable powers of concentration. Although they are good with details, they tend to be on the conservative side and aren't always adaptable.

GEMINI: Those born under the sign of the Twins tend to prefer to make money by brilliant schemes instead of working steadily and acting on long-term plans. They don't like criticism of their work. However, they know how to make others feel at ease.

CANCER: Cancer people are conscientious, earnest, and thorough in their work. They are characterized by their patience, persistence, and attention to detail. Their general dislike for waste and carelessness makes them good workers.

LEO: Those born under the sign of the Lion handle positions of authority well and like to find themselves in jobs where the chance to exercise their ability to manage exists. While Leo people are natural-born leaders, they are often critical to a fault.

VIRGO: Virgo people are exceptionally industrious and hardworking. They have a flair for detailed work, yet are sometimes materialistic. Virgos are very often too critical, expecting others to have their standard of devotion to hard work.

LIBRA: Librans make good business partners, yet tend to be on the conservative side. Because they consider matters from all angles before making a decision, they are good at analyzing any situation. Librans are particular about money matters, yet won't hoard money once they've earned it.

SCORPIO: Those born under the sign of the Scorpion love power, and their many abilities help them achieve high positions. They get right to the heart of any matter and face facts. Although strictly honest in their work, they are often dominating and authoritative.

SAGITTARIUS: Sagittarians are well suited to business, being capable workers and loyal to their employers. They don't like petty detail work, rather they prefer jobs which give plenty of scope for their expression and talent.

CAPRICORN: Capricorn people have great understanding and patience in their work. Their capacity for self-discipline, honesty, and stability drives them to be successful in whatever they do. Above all, respect is important.

AQUARIUS: Aquarians' inventive and progressive minds like to break from the conventional, yet they always remain efficient and dedicated. Count on Aquarians to be trustworthy, honest, and averse to arguments.

PISCES: Those born under the sign of the Fish are earnest and honest, but often have difficulty making decisions. Although Pisces people are generally good workers, they are wary of accepting responsibility.

No sooner had Jennifer hung up the phone than it rang again. "One more minute, Dad."

Her heart gave an extra beat when she heard Danny's voice on the other end of the line.

"I know it's been a while, but I was hoping I could come to see you—just for a minute or two."

"Tonight?"

"Yeah, is that okay?"

Jennifer hesitated. Why did he want to come over ...unless...? She remembered how they had planned it the year before, applying for the internships together.

"It'll be perfect," Jennifer had said dreamily. "We'll spend every minute together. And my parents won't object."

It hadn't worked out that way. But maybe now that they were actually working together....

"Danny...is it the *Chronicle*?

"Yeah." Danny sounded surprised. "How'd you know?"

"Call it woman's intuition." Jennifer's heart leapt—he did remember. He wanted to clear things up between them and make a fresh start.

"Jen? You there?"

"Yes...when will you come?"

"Ten minutes, if it's okay. Tell your folks I won't stay long, promise."

"Don't worry about that, they always liked you," she added warmly.

"Right. Okay then, ten minutes."

Jennifer flew. She ran downstairs and begged her father to postpone their review. She changed into a different blouse. Her hair was hopeless. She tucked it behind her ears and then shook it loose again—Danny liked it better loose. She was reaching for her blusher when the doorbell rang. She closed her eyes and forced herself to be calm. She heard Danny greet her father, and her father called up to her to say Danny was there.

"Okay, I'm coming."

Taking a deep breath, Jennifer walked gracefully down the stairs.

"Jen, hi." He stood as she entered the room.

"Hi." She kept her voice as casual as his, throwing her father an impatient look. Finally he excused himself and she and Danny were alone.

"Well, long time," Danny said. He rubbed his hands together nervously and Jennifer felt a flood of affection for him.

"Too long," she said softly.

"Well, Jen, I . . ."

"I remembered too," Jennifer said as he struggled for words. For the first time in months she looked directly into his eyes. "A team—remember? We already did almost everything together; the *Chronicle* would be the final touch. Working side by side."

Danny seemed a bit stunned—he was so emotional, Jennifer thought. So sweet and even naive sometimes . . . those little-boy eyes. She stepped closer and Danny lifted his arms automatically. She fit right inside—like always. She put her arms around him and kissed him.

It was a lovely soft kiss—the kiss of people parted for a while but longing to be together again.

Danny stared at her, his face slightly flushed. Finally he cleared his throat and spoke with difficulty.

"Nice . . . what made you do that?"

"You're so sweet, to remember."

"Remember?"

"Us, our plans." Jennifer gazed at him. "Our team, of course."

"Team—sure, right."

Jennifer drew back. She pushed his arms away.

"Danny—wait a minute. What *are* you doing here?"

"Like you said, the paper." He shrugged helplessly. "I had a story idea..."

"A story?"

"I need some help."

"You want me to help you on a story."

"Yeah, in a way. Actually, it's your sister..."

"Adele?"

"Didn't she do a research paper on Collingwood's history? I thought a series would be perfect for the *Chronicle*. I can whip up an outline, but I thought I'd read Adele's paper first. Is it here, or could I call her? What's her number?" Danny fumbled through his pockets for a pencil and paper.

"You want Adele's number?" Jennifer's eyes blazed.

"Yeah, at college. I don't have it."

"You came all the way over here to ask for my sister's phone number?"

"I would've asked on the phone, but this is more polite."

"Polite! You're worried about manners when you burst in here and insult me?"

"I didn't insult you. You didn't write the paper I need."

"You kissed me," Jennifer said bitterly, "when you didn't mean it."

"You kissed me, actually."

Jennifer snatched his pencil and paper and threw them on the floor. "I thought you came here to make up," she said fiercely. "You shouldn't have kissed me."

"I'm not crazy," he said. "Who wouldn't kiss you?"

She pushed him toward the door. "How dare you . . . you

skunk . . . how dare you use me to get to my sister . . ."

"Wait, Jen—"

"Get out of here. I never want to see you again."

"You'll see me at the paper tomorrow."

"Well, don't talk to me. From now on, it's war between us. Get out."

"Don't get hysterical, Jen—"

She pushed him out the door and slammed it hard.

"That's it," she said through clenched teeth. "It's done, finished. No way will it work out. I'll never look at him again."

"Jennifer, how about your quiz?" Her father poked his head out from the kitchen.

"Oh, Daddy, not now." Jennifer fled up the stairs, safely shutting her door behind her before bursting into angry, miserable tears.

—

_____ 7 ★

Saturday morning there was the first hint of frost in the air. Cathy changed her light cotton shirt for a sweater. It was a shame to waste such sparkling sunshine on a day indoors at the mall, but more stores had signed up for the Starscope promotion and Cathy couldn't wait to get the project into full swing. She, Elizabeth, and Jessica would run the first shift at the mall. Will had already taught them the simple commands to run the program.

She managed to swallow a decent breakfast and be ready when Jim's car pulled up in front of the house.

"Cathy, wait!" Jane flew out the front door toward the car. Jim braked.

"What now?" Cathy grumbled. "If she wants to come with us, somebody please tell her no."

But it wasn't a free ride Jane was after. "It's the *Chronicle* calling," Jane said breathlessly. "They said it was urgent and that I should stop you if I could."

"We don't have time to stop, Cath." Jessica checked her watch. "We have to get there before the stores open."

Cathy hesitated.

"Urgent," Jane repeated.

"Okay, I'm coming. Wait for me, you guys. I'll hurry."

Charlie Ahearn was on the phone. "We've an emergency," he explained. A child had been reported missing overnight in nearby Willburn. "There's an all-out search going on, and the *Chronicle* needs people on the spot. We're using all our regular stringers, plus you interns. When can you be at the office?"

Cathy's mind raced. Starscope was her responsibility but . . . there was a story to get. Jennifer wouldn't hesitate. And if Jennifer was with the group that found the child, she was practically guaranteed a story. Maybe front page. If Cathy was serious about being a reporter and showing the Academy kids she had what it takes, she had no choice.

"Cathy, are you there?"

"I can be at the *Chronicle* in ten minutes. Do I need to bring anything?"

"Usual notebook and pencil."

"Okay. I'll be there."

"Anything wrong?" Jane stood in the doorway.

"Tell Mom I need a ride to the *Chronicle* right away. I'll be back in a minute."

The walk to Jim's car seemed to take longer than it should have. Cathy found her friends puzzled and impatient when she didn't get in the car.

"What do you mean you can't come?" Jessica looked at Elizabeth. "What does she mean?"

"Cathy, you organized this whole thing. You've got to show—it's the first day. We can't face all those people alone. You're the brave one. I hate talking to strangers." Elizabeth's eyes pleaded with her.

"Think of it as a sacred duty." Cathy saw her mother heading for the garage. "I can't lose the internship. And I will if I don't show up. Besides, do you want an Academy kid to scoop me on this story?"

"Who cares?" Jessica said. "I could have done other things today too, you know."

"Elizabeth," Cathy begged, "you understand, don't you? You see why I have to go."

"I'd rather you came with us, but I guess I see your point. The *Chronicle* is depending on you. If you have to go, you have to go."

"Thanks. Tell the others I'm really sorry. I'll get the best story out of this. You'll all be proud of me, I promise."

Behind them, Cathy's mother was pulling the car out of the driveway. Cathy paused. "Good luck," was all she could say. Elizabeth waved as Jim pulled away from the curb, and Cathy hurried to her mother's car.

"I hope I get a story out of this," she said grimly. "I may have lost my friends."

"You're a reporter now," her mother told her. "And a good reporter follows her story."

The Willburn County Courthouse was the center of the lost-child operation. Besides the police, an army of citizens had volunteered to join the search parties combing the thick woods.

"This has happened before," Charlie Ahearn told Cathy and Jennifer. "It was a terrible thing, a kidnapping. But even if this is a simple case of a little girl wandering off by herself, it could mean trouble. These woods are treacherous. There's a million places to get lost, to fall down, to get trapped. She's only five years old," he paused. "I have kids of my own.

"I hate to say this," he continued, "but tragedy sells newspapers. If the worst happens, we'll be lucky to have someone here as an eyewitness. I just hope that someone isn't one of you girls."

Cathy hoped so too.

"Where's Danny Burns?" Jennifer scanned the courthouse for a sign of his lanky frame. "He isn't already out with a search party, is he?"

Charlie was scribbling instructions for the girls. "Burns? No, I couldn't reach him this morning. His mother said he was out playing tennis. We'll manage without him."

Cathy took the directions, which included phone numbers to call throughout the day. As soon as she was alone with Jennifer, she confided in dismay, "He isn't here! Do you know what I gave up this morning?" She quickly told Jennifer about Starscope. "Everyone was furious with me and now I find out Danny didn't come at all! Nothing would have happened to me if I didn't come when they called."

Jennifer looked at her like she couldn't believe her ears. "Are you crazy? Who cares about the Zodiacs? Don't you realize what we've got here?"

"A lost kid, I know—it's terrible. And it's a big story."

Jennifer shook her head in exasperation. "Big story— it's a scoop! We just beat Burns at his own game without even trying. Cathy, don't even think about that stupid mall project of yours. This is a thousand times more important."

"I know, but all my friends . . ." Cathy looked doubtful.

"Some journalist you are." Jennifer chuckled.

"You're gloating," Cathy said, surprised.

"Of course I'm gloating. I just hope I'm the one there when they find this kid. And even though I hope she's okay, what I really want most is a good story."

"Jennifer!" Cathy was truly shocked. "Don't you think that's carrying things too far?"

"I think I'm being professional. Wise up, Cathy. I'm not happy this kid is lost, but probably nothing awful will happen. It isn't another kidnapping. But it is a chance to beat out Danny Burns. And if you think I feel sorry about your friends, forget it. Danny Burns deserves anything he gets. I mean for him to take it personally this time. Come on, Cathy—you should try to scoop me, too."

"Look," Cathy said, "I want a byline story. But just between us, I also want friends. I can't be ruthless."

"Don't worry." Jennifer smiled. "I know where to draw the line. With you, it's fair competition. But with Danny Burns, it's war."

"I get it," Cathy said. "Let the best reporter win."

They shook hands, but Cathy was puzzled.

"Jennifer, don't you care about Danny anymore?"

"Not right now," she said.

When Cathy went to get a cup of coffee, Jennifer pulled a folded piece of paper from her jeans pocket. She had found the letter in its neatly addressed envelope in her mailbox the day after Danny came to visit. It was a letter of apology. Danny explained that he really came over because deep down, he wanted to see her again—kiss her again. She wasn't going to believe him.

Cathy was right about one thing, Jennifer thought as she refolded the letter. I am stubborn. And I hate to lose. First I'll even the score between Danny and me. Then I'll decide if I still care.

It was nine-thirty by the time the first search parties came back to the courthouse. The girls were assigned to patrol cars where one officer was part of the search party. The interns had to wait with the second officer in the car, to be the first to hear the news. Cathy was assigned to wait with Officer Jim Nivins. He was a family man, and he was upset by the search detail.

"You may think this is boring, sitting in the car like this," he told Cathy after the first hour had dragged by. "But it's important. We're the link here. If they get the kid, we're on the spot faster than any ambulance. Her life could depend on us."

Cathy had a sudden inspiration. "Could I interview you?"

Patrolman Nivins gazed at her in surprise.

"You know, a behind-the-scenes look at the cop on the job."

Nivins looked doubtful. "No one wants to read about me."

But Cathy insisted. As the policeman began to talk, Cathy secretly congratulated herself on her fast thinking. The human-interest angle was surely a crowd pleaser. As Nivins talked the hours went by more quickly. By noontime, when they were relieved by another patrol car, Cathy had enough information about the daily life of a policeman to write a three-week series. She couldn't wait to tell Jennifer. But something stopped her. What if Jennifer copied her idea? What if Jennifer's was better?

As Jennifer approached her, Cathy quickly tucked her notebook away in her pocketbook.

"Pretty boring after all, isn't it?" Jennifer grinned. "Here, I got you the thickest sandwich they had." She held it out and Cathy took it gratefully.

"I'm starved." She bit down hungrily, ignoring the pang of guilt she felt. She didn't dare ask Jennifer any questions. If Jennifer hadn't come up with a way to make the day less boring, Cathy couldn't help her. Cathy was relieved when they parted to go back to their assignments. Jennifer reached out to pat her arm.

"Don't look so glum. There may be news any minute. That thought should keep you from being bored."

Cathy bit her tongue. She felt like a cheat. Although Jennifer might have approved of what Cathy was doing, Cathy felt sneaky, not clever.

Another hour of waiting went by. Patrolman Nivins was explaining his training when the call came through. The little girl had been found safe and unharmed.

"They're bringing her to the hospital now," she reported breathlessly to Mr. Ahearn. She read all the remaining facts from her notes.

"Your story checks out," he told her. "Thanks, Cathy. You did a great job."

"Should I write it up now? What's the deadline?"

"I'm sorry, you misunderstood. That's my job. But I couldn't have done it without your information. This won't be a major story since there was no foul play involved and the child is unharmed. I know how eager you are to get something in print, and you'll get a chance." He patted her shoulder kindly. "Why don't you find Jennifer and I'll get you both back to the *Chronicle*."

"I heard," Jennifer said before Cathy spoke. "I guess we both got our hopes up too high."

"Easy come, easy go. Hey..." Cathy's eyes lit up. "Maybe we can make it to the mall. You could come with me and meet everyone."

"I'd like that a lot."

It was a long ride from Willburn. As Jennifer pumped Mr. Ahearn for stories about the *Chronicle*, Cathy sat silently wondering if she should confide in Jennifer. She felt foolish and ashamed at once. Not only had she gotten her hopes up ridiculously high, her clever idea had become a burden.

"Jennifer..." Cathy pulled her away from the parking lot. "Before we go, I have something to tell you."

"What?"

"I know you said friendship is separate from competition, but I did something that bothers me."

"Does it have to do with Danny? Maybe we should go somewhere and sit down," Jennifer interrupted.

"No, it won't take long," Cathy protested, but she followed Jennifer down the block to the diner.

They found an empty booth and ordered Cokes and fries.

"Now tell me."

Cathy began, "While we were sitting around waiting, I thought, wouldn't it be great to have an exclusive interview with one of the policemen at the scene. You know, human-interest stuff about the face behind the badge. So I interviewed Patrolman Nivins."

Jennifer tore the wrapping from her straw and waited for Cathy to continue.

"The thing is, when I saw you at lunchtime, I was afraid if I told you, you might steal the idea. I thought I would lose an exclusive story. Maybe that's what a real reporter would do, but I feel lousy about it."

"You do, huh?" Jennifer pushed her straw around her glass slowly.

"Of course. I didn't trust you enough to confide in you. I was brought up to trust friends—or else it isn't friendship. It wasn't honest."

"If you hadn't told me now, I would never have known," Jennifer pointed out.

Cathy shrugged. "I'm no good at guilt. I don't want to win that way."

Jennifer set her glass down with a thud on the tabletop. "You make me feel like a real rat."

"You? Why?"

Jennifer looked at Cathy. "You think you're the only one with a clever idea?" She tapped herself on the chest. "I have my own secret. I had a scoop all lined up too."

"What? When?"

"At lunch—same as you. The difference is, I wasn't going to tell you about it. Ever."

"What difference does it make now?" Cathy said.

"It makes a difference—you know it," Jennifer replied. "You're a nice person. I'm not so nice. I wanted to beat you out for a story—friend or not."

They sat silently.

"Cathy, it's no excuse, but I told you—my family has the pressure on tight. I have to be the best. But it's not just my family—*I* want to be."

"You've told me."

"If it helps to know, I admire you. I'd even like to be more like you. And less like me."

Cathy shrugged.

"Are we friends?" Jennifer asked hopefully.

"I'm not used to seeing Jennifer Chow humble. If you can accept me, I can accept you."

"I've never had a friend like you." Jennifer smiled. "It feels great."

Cathy hesitated only a second. "As long as you're feeling so good, what was your idea?"

"There didn't seem much point in hanging around the patrol car for so long. I managed to get to the little girl's house! I got in and actually interviewed the mother."

Cathy gasped.

"She seemed grateful to talk," Jennifer continued. "I guess talking to a sixteen-year-old wasn't like talking to an adult. She showed me pictures of the kids growing up. We almost had a good time—except for her being worried to death. I got an interesting story."

"I'll bet you did." Cathy was in awe. "What nerve."

Jennifer shrugged. "What could be more interesting than what the mother was going through? I was there when they got the call, too—that the kid was all right. They tore out of that house so fast . . . it's too bad I couldn't go to the hospital with them." Jennifer's smile was wistful. "What a story that would make."

"Talk about a nose for news! I thought a Taurus wasn't outgoing."

"I am shy," Jennifer protested. "It's just that I'm ambitious."

"You're shy like a bulldozer." Cathy fished out the longest french fry, chewing thoughtfully. Her eyes narrowed. "Our stories would make good human-interest features, don't you think?"

"They aren't front-page news."

"Still, the mother's agony, the concerned patrolman, and a big happy ending. I can see it now—a huge picture of the mother hugging her little girl and the policeman who helped them. Isn't that local news?"

"I like it," Jennifer announced. "Let's write it and bring it to Mrs. Mead on Monday."

"You mean, work together—a team?"

"Why not?" Jennifer grinned. "Or are you too competitive to share a byline with me?"

"You're on." Cathy shook Jennifer's hand, sealing the deal.

"Wait. Before we do anything stupid, let's go ask Mr. Ahearn if it's a good idea. No use getting our hopes up again."

"If he likes it, we'll have to get started."

"Right away. You realize that means no time for the mall."

"I didn't. Will it take that long?"

"Are you kidding? We'll have to work tonight and all day tomorrow too."

"And I've got a chemistry test Monday. How can I get to the mall, write the article, and still study? And a bunch of kids are getting together tonight at J.L.'s."

Jennifer eyed her coolly. "You can't go—no way. Make a choice."

Cathy hesitated.

"Look, we can study together when the article's done. I had chemistry already and I got straight A's."

"But Starscope was my idea. And the club..."

"They'll understand."

"Starscope can get along without me for a while. I'll just have to put in an appearance tomorrow. The kids'll understand."

"All right!"

"See, Jennifer," Cathy said happily. "We don't always have to compete."

"I think I'm going to like this team."

They linked arms and left the diner smiling.

_____ 8 ★

"At last—relief!" Jessica cheered as the other girls finally returned from their lunch break. "What took you so long? I thought we'd go crazy waiting for you to get back."

"Tell me about it," J.L. answered. "I was bored enough this morning."

"I see business is jumping," Mara cracked.

Except for the Zodiac members, the area around the Starscope table was deserted.

"How many have we sold altogether?" J.L. asked.

"Twenty-seven."

"How many not counting family and friends?" Penny sat down with a thud on a nearby bench.

Jessica scowled at her. "I'm not counting. And if you think this is good publicity..."

"And it's worse for charity," J.L. finished. "What have we cleared? Fifteen bucks? Forget it."

"I don't get it," Abby said. "We told everyone at school. We put posters all around the mall. What else can we do?"

"Oh, no—here comes Coffman to check up on us."

"Abby?" Will appealed to the most levelheaded one at the table. "Is it really that bad?"

"Numbers don't lie," she replied. "Our worthy Zodiac project is a giant bust. We'll stick it out the rest of the day, but I don't see any point in coming back tomorrow."

"You're not a quitter. Maybe it'll pick up."

"I can't see why. I don't know what to do to get this thing rolling."

"Cathy should be here," Will said. "The idea sounded great when she came up with it. I bet she'd know how to turn things around."

"Your beloved Cathy has deserted us," Jessica pointed out. "Supergirl Rosen couldn't fix this mess. If she had any loyalty to us, she'd have shown up by now."

"Great logic, Jess," Abby chided.

"I don't care." Jessica pouted. "Cathy thought of this. It's her responsibility too. I feel ridiculous, sitting here for everyone to stare at."

"Don't blame Cathy that you're ridiculous," J.L. snapped.

"This time it's her fault," Jessica retorted.

"Let's not start fighting. Maybe we should quit now. The Zodiacs can easily come up with another cause," Abby said.

"Maybe we should. And we should forget tonight too," Jessica said angrily.

"Cathy isn't responsible for bad sales." J.L. rushed to Cathy's defense.

"How do we know that?"

"Hey, Coffman!" someone yelled. "Is that you?"

All heads turned as a boy strode into view.

"Danny Burns!" Will called out. "It's good to see my old camp buddy. How's the Academy treating you?"

"Who is that?" Elizabeth whispered.

"Yes—who?" Jessica breathed.

"Hold on, girl—I don't like the gleam in your eye," Abby warned.

"That's no gleam, that's a leer," J.L. corrected.

Jessica walked quickly to Will's side, considerably perkier than she was a minute before. "Aren't you going to introduce me to your friend?" She smiled invitingly at Danny.

"So we can sell him a Starscope?"

J.L. whispered to Abby, "She's actually batting her eyelashes. I may be sick."

"She's not subtle," Abby whispered back. "She sometimes scares off more boys in a day than I meet in a month."

J.L. shook her head in disbelief.

Will pushed his glasses into place, suddenly uncomfortable as Jessica linked her arm through his.

"Any friend of Will's is a friend of mine." She cocked her head to one side, flirting shamelessly.

"Danny Burns, Jessica Holly." Will untangled Jessica. "D.B., I hear you're on the *Chronicle* with my girlfriend, Cathy. She told me all about it."

"You're *that* Danny Burns?" Jessica stared at him. "I thought all the interns were at the search."

"What search?" Danny finally looked at Jessica.

"Don't you know?" Jessica's green eyes widened in astonishment. "Cathy couldn't be here because this little girl got lost and everyone from the *Chronicle* drove out to Willburn to cover the story."

Danny looked stunned. "They did?"

"Cathy went, and that girl Jennifer too."

"Jennifer Chow?"

"Yes."

Elizabeth walked over. "Jess is right. It was an emergency."

Danny groaned. "I blew it." He dropped his head into his hands.

In a flash, Jessica was at his side, patting his shoulder. "It couldn't be that important," she crooned.

"Oh no? It's just the first real story to break while I've been at the paper. And both those girls have a shot at a great story. I could kick myself for being at the tennis court." He shook his head in dismay. "Round One goes to Rosen and Chow. I bet the two of them are eating this up."

"I don't see what's so important," Jessica protested. "There'll be other stories, won't there?"

"I just lost big points with the editor."

Jessica tossed her head. "Kids get lost all the time. Find something better to write about."

"Like what, for instance?"

"Me, for instance." Jessica eagerly pulled a chair up next to Danny's. "Write about the typical teenage girl in between boyfriends."

"No offense, but I think a lost kid is better than that."

"Then write about the Zodiacs. We need publicity. Write about this event to raise money for a worthy cause."

Danny looked around him. "What event?"

Jessica and Will explained about the Starscope program. "It was Cathy's idea to sell the horoscopes to raise money. Computer Capers, we hope, will get publicity, too."

Danny frowned. "Cathy Rosen thought of it? And she isn't here?"

"She had to go when her editor called," Abby said loyally. "Anyway, this has turned into a big failure."

"You're going about getting publicity wrong," Danny said. "You need a good front man, someone lively to pull in the crowds. You need a giveaway." He reeled off ideas absentmindedly. "Circulate through the mall, hand out a few free horoscopes, and other people will want them too. Call attention to yourselves—don't just sit here. That will get you noticed, and that will get you publicity."

Abby and J.L. exchanged glances. "He's right."

"Where were you when we needed you?" Jessica moaned.

"I'm here now." Danny sprang up, taking a good look at the Starscope table. "Turn this table around. Pull it out so people can see you. We'll get this thing going. I'll let you in on a little secret." He tugged at one end of the table while J.L. grabbed the other. "People are attracted to success. Act successful and they'll swamp you with business. I'll tell you something else, too."

"What's that?" Jessica's eyes filled with adoration.

"You don't sit around and wait for publicity. You create it. What you need is newspaper coverage. And I just happen to be the man to get it for you."

"Danny! What a wonderful idea," Jessica crowed.

"Are you serious?" Abby approached Danny. "Can you get the *Chronicle* to do a story about us?"

"I'll give it a try. It's their type of story—local businesses pulling together to raise money for charity. Pretty girls— it's a natural. Why don't some of you come with me. We'll cover the mall the way I said. Then I'll get a few of the facts and write it up. Will you girls be here tomorrow?"

"Yes," Abby answered for all of them, enthusiastic again. "I think we can pull this off after all."

"Sure you can." Danny grinned at them. "And I'm going to beat my colleagues at their own game. Remember this— advertising sells newspapers, not lost children. With the right publicity, every merchant in the mall will support this project. I guarantee it. This place will be hopping."

"Danny Burns," Abby said sincerely, "you just saved our lives. The Zodiac Club owes you for this."

"You scratch my back, I'll scratch yours," Danny answered slyly.

"I'll do more than scratch your back," Jessica exclaimed, reaching up quickly to grab Danny's head between her hands. Then—"I'm sorry," she said innocently. "I don't know what came over me."

Danny didn't react. Instead, he grabbed a handful of Starscope charts from the table, pointing to Elizabeth, Penny, and Mara. "Come with me," he said. "I'll show you how to work a crowd."

Abby watched them go. "Do you think he can do what he says he can do, Will?"

"Danny has his own magic. He just might be back with a line of customers."

"He does have magic." Jessica's eyes glistened. "Do you think he noticed me?"

"Just possibly," J.L. drawled.

"Won't Cathy be sorry she missed this." Jessica licked her lips with glee. "She should have thought of it herself. She's our friend—she could have written about Starscope. But she had more important things to do."

Abby fidgeted uneasily at the computer. "She'll be here tomorrow."

"You think so? I think she's in love with that newspaper now. The Zodiacs are the farthest thing from her mind."

"I could use a break." Cathy stretched her arms over her head, pulling out the kinks in her back. "Could we take some time off, Jennifer?"

Jennifer frowned. "We've got lots to do."

"But we could zip over to J.L.'s."

"Don't worry about your friends. They'll understand."

"I'll just put in an appearance and you can meet my friends. We'll get right back here—promise."

"You say an hour—what if it's more?"

"You can drag me away, screaming."

"I wouldn't ordinarily . . ."

Cathy smiled. "Please?"

"One hour."

"Spoken like a true fairy godmother. Come on."

Jennifer whipped around the curves leading to J.L.'s house.

"Don't speed on my account."

Jennifer glanced at her and they both laughed—it was exhilarating to be out, fresh air filling the car, music blaring.

"You sure know how to mix work with pleasure," Cathy said to her new friend.

"Thanks."

J.L.'s impressive house came into view. The wrought-iron gates were open and cars were parked along the circular driveway. Jennifer left the Toyota last in line, and the two girls hurried toward a side room where the sound of music blared.

"You meant it when you said J.L. was super rich." Jennifer scanned the house and grounds, taking it all in. "Impressive."

"And she throws a great party."

"Cathy!" Abby hurried over to them as they stepped into the noisy room. "I thought you wouldn't make it."

"Had to come to my friend's house." Cathy grinned. She pulled Jennifer to her side. "This is Jennifer Chow—Academy girl."

"The competition?" Abby grinned and led them to a corner where Elizabeth and J.L. were adding new bags of potato chips and pretzels to empty bowls. The girls were introduced all around.

"Why are you late?" J.L. asked.

Jennifer poked Cathy in the ribs, shaking her head frantically.

"We're working—" Cathy stopped in mid-sentence.

Jennifer's eyes turned toward the door. Cathy turned and saw Danny Burns, arms filled with cans of cold drinks, following Will down the steps.

"—on an assignment," Cathy finished lamely.

Danny stopped in surprise, seeing Jennifer. He deposited the cans on a table and came to her side.

"You get around," he remarked. "Part of the crowd now?"

"How about you," Jennifer retorted. "Since when do you know these people?"

They glared at each other.

"Danny's been at—" J.L. started to say.

"We all know each other, that's all," Danny interrupted quickly. He shot J.L. a warning look, and she realized he meant to keep his involvement in Starscope a secret.

"Great," Jennifer said, smiling icily at him. Danny turned away to open a can and Jennifer pulled Cathy aside.

"We can't stay. I'm not comfortable here."

"I won't say a word about our story," Cathy whispered. "Not to anyone. Danny won't find out."

"I still don't like being here."

"I have to stay. I have to explain that I couldn't do the Starscope thing today."

"We should get back to work."

"Let me just see Will—then we can go."

But Will was deep in a verbal contest with Danny. Jessica, and a bunch of kids were watching and laughing. Finally Cathy pulled Abby's arm. "I'm trying to explain," she yelled above the noise. "Listen, Abby, no one's mad at me, are they? For missing Starscope today?"

Abby shrugged. "They're not thrilled, obviously. I tried to stick up for you—I know your internship is important.

But it's a good thing you're coming tomorrow."

"Would they resent me if I didn't show?" Cathy said lightly.

Abby laughed. "Are you kidding? It was your idea."

Jennifer was at Cathy's side. "Can we go? Mr. Popularity Burns really makes me sick—he always has to be the big shot," she said in disgust.

"Let's wait just a few more minutes," Cathy urged. She had a terribly uneasy feeling. "I really want to explain things to Will . . ."

Jennifer turned aside. She searched through her pock-etbook and found a pencil. Then she took out the note Danny had written her—the apology. "No, thanks," she scrawled across the top of the letter, folding it up again. She joined the circle of kids gathered around Will and Danny.

Jennifer looked at the expression on Jessica's face—pure idol worship, she thought. She pushed through the crowd, grabbed Jessica's hand, and thrust the crumpled-up note into it.

"Give this to Burns," she said. "I'll be outside," she told Cathy.

"I give up," Will cried, throwing his hands into the air.

Danny beamed. "Knew you couldn't take it!"

"This is for you." Jessica wrinkled her nose at the crum-pled note in her hand and passed it to Danny.

"Huh?" He took the paper idly, enjoying his success, and unfolded it. His smile faltered when he read "No, thanks" and realized what it was.

"You were great," Jessica watched him in admiration.

Someone put on a new record—a slow song. Danny recognized it as one of Jennifer's favorites—they had danced to it before their final fight. Hearing it now, Jennifer stopped on her way outside, turning back just in time to see Danny enfold Jessica in his arms.

Jennifer ran for her car.

Cathy had started to follow Will down the stairs. "He's in the bathroom," Jim Newman said as he waited on line.

She walked back to look for J.L. or Abby. The first thing she saw was Danny and Jessica clasped together.

"Oh no," she muttered, realizing Jennifer was nowhere in sight. "Abby," she called, "I've got to go. I'll call you tomorrow, okay?"

She sprinted from the room, calling Jennifer's name as she ran down the driveway.

"Thanks for coming to my party," J.L. said sarcastically, watching her go. "Here's to Starscope."

"Great party, J.L.," Danny called to her.

J.L. smiled in pleasure. "Well, it's nice to be appreciated."

---

9 ★

Cathy rolled over in bed and groaned.

"Eight o'clock, Cathy," her mother called. "You wanted to be up on time today."

"Okay," Cathy grumbled, then sat up straight in bed. "I promised I'd call Jennifer first thing."

Her mother leaned in the doorway. "How did the writing go last night? You kids were still at work when Dad and I went to sleep."

"Great." Cathy flung her arms around her knees. "Jen is a genius at organizing facts. And the word processor really helped. If I do say so myself, I think it's good."

"I'm glad to see you excited about this—but don't neglect your other work."

"Hurry up—I need the bathroom, Jane," Cathy yelled. "I've got a lot to do."

"Are you going to the mall?" Jane patted her mouth with a fluffy towel. "Some of the kids said your Zodiac project was really going strong. I'm going back today—everyone is getting horoscopes."

"Maybe this afternoon. I don't know," she finished vaguely. "I'll call Abby and see if I can get out of it."

The phone rang before Cathy could dial Abby's number. It was Jennifer.

"Is it too early to start?" Jennifer sounded wide-awake. "I got this fabulous idea. What if we arrange our material like a documentary? We could have headlines: 'SATURDAY, 6:00 A.M.'—then describe what the mother was going through and how the police were handling the search at that point. That would get us right inside the police station."

"Brilliant! I couldn't think of a way to get all the police activity in."

"Are we geniuses? I can't wait to show this to Mrs. Mead."

"Me either—especially since Charlie Ahearn liked the idea so much. Come over right away. Tell your folks it's fine for you to eat here."

"Great," Jennifer said. "See you."

Cathy flew downstairs to gobble some breakfast. She returned to her computer and called up their rough draft on the screen. She searched for logical places to insert their time-of-day headlines.

She forgot what time of day it was herself. She'd call Abby later.

Abby and Elizabeth hurried to their lockers, pushing through the crowded hallway.

"Why are Mondays always like this?" Abby complained, tripping over someone's foot. She stopped to chat with three girls on the field-hockey team who wanted to recruit her.

"Hey, homeroom, remember?" Elizabeth tugged at Abby's arm.

"Thanks for rescuing me. I'd like to join the team, but I don't have time for every activity."

"Especially not now. Operation Starscope is really a hit. We're making hundreds of dollars in profits." Elizabeth beamed.

"We did it."

"Danny Burns did it," Elizabeth corrected. "I don't know where we'd be without him."

"He really is incredible." Abby stopped for a quick drink at the fountain, delayed by more kids calling hello. "He's a dynamic person."

"Are you interested in him?" Elizabeth studied her friend carefully. "I know Buddy is away at college, but is Danny Burns your type?"

"I looked him up in my horoscope book," Abby began.

"And?"

"No surprise." Abby let out an exaggerated sigh. "Remember—Will Coffman is a Taurus. I've never gotten vibes from Will."

"Will is Cathy's boyfriend. Besides, you'd never be attracted to Will."

"Danny Burns does have more spark than Will," Abby mused. "I like his energy."

"Abby Martin, tell me the truth. Do you like Danny Burns?"

"No." Abby grinned. "Adjacent signs don't get along romantically. We're too much alike."

"And besides, Jessica would kill you if you said you liked Danny. She has him staked out for herself," Elizabeth finished wisely.

"Danny Burns isn't interested in her, I can tell you that."

"Why? Don't Virgo and Taurus get along?"

"They do, but not Jessica and Danny." Abby leaned against her locker. "Danny likes attention as much as Jessica. I don't think that's Jess's idea of the perfect mate."

"Maybe you should tell Jess that, before she goes too far. She has herself convinced Danny Burns was flirting with her."

Abby frowned. "He wasn't—no more than with anyone else. Anyone could see that. I hope Jess isn't serious about him."

"There's nothing we can do about it if she is. We can't stop her from liking him."

"No. And I can see why she likes him. Maybe it will work out this time. She's never had a steady boyfriend and she's really a great kid."

Elizabeth raised her eyebrows. "Overly enthusiastic," she said, "but good at heart. If only she'd relax and let some boy get to know the real Jessica—let her sweet side show a little more. She wouldn't have any trouble at all."

"Then she wouldn't be our Jess."

"I guess not." Elizabeth opened her own locker. "Speaking of Monday mornings—can you believe I've got an English essay due first period? I wrote it in about half an hour last night. Starscope is really taking up more time than I thought." She stifled a yawn. "We could have used some help yesterday. Too bad Cathy never showed. She didn't call you?"

Abby shook her head. "I'm really mad at her. I can't believe she wasn't curious about how we were doing. And we sure could have used her help."

"I hate to say this, but the others are really angry."

"I know. I heard. But I'm sure she has a good explanation. She's never let me down before."

"Tell that to J.L. and Penny. And Mara took it personally. They haven't known Cathy as long as we have. They don't know it's not like her to do this kind of thing."

"Cathy will have an explanation."

Cathy didn't even see Penny and J.L. as she hurried along the hall, her head bent over her chemistry book. The warning bell had already rung. Cathy had overslept, missed breakfast, and missed a ride to school with her mother. The bus arrived late and, in her rush to get to homeroom, she had taken the wrong books from her locker and lost precious minutes going back to exchange them.

"Cathy," J.L. called.

Cathy walked right by.

"Some apology that was." Penny stared down the hall after Cathy.

J.L. frowned. "She didn't seem too worried about us, did she?"

"At least she could say hello."

"If that's how she wants it, we can play the same game." J.L. hid her hurt feelings behind a cool smile. "If she doesn't see us, we won't see her."

"Right," Penny agreed. "No one talks to Cathy at all."

"I expected better from her. Now she's only pals with Academy kids."

* * *

Cathy's chemistry class wasn't until after lunch, but there was little time to study. She knew she had been stupid to wait until the last minute to study for her test. If only they had studied in the middle of the day, when her mind was still fresh. But Cathy had persuaded Jen to leave the chemistry until after dinner. By the time they had finished a good draft of the article, proofread it for spelling errors one more time, had dinner and printed a copy of the article, Cathy was too tired to think straight. Jennifer's careful explanations had only confused her.

In the middle of the night, Cathy woke up with the sickening realization that she had forgotten about an entire chapter of her textbook. She would flunk for sure. Unable to get back to sleep, Cathy dragged out her chemistry text and tried to cram the last chapter, but it was hopeless. If she could memorize a few facts by sixth period, she might be saved—but so far, her teachers demanded her attention in every class. She would have to cram during lunchtime. If she flunked a major chemistry test, it would take all trimester to pull her grade up. If her grades dropped, she wouldn't be able to continue as an intern at the *Chronicle*.

The morning crawled by. With grim determination Cathy marched into the cafeteria at lunchtime, bought yogurt and an apple, and hid herself in a corner, her chemistry books spread out in front of her.

"Cath, what gives?" Will slid into the seat beside hers.

Cathy groaned. "Not now, Will. I don't have time." She stared at the atom diagrams in front of her. They swam before her eyes. "I've got to concentrate. I can't talk to anyone."

"Yeah—well, no one's talking to you anyway."

"Please, Will."

"Hey, listen." Will put his hand over her chemistry book. "Your friends are pretty mad at you. They think you might have something to say to them."

At a table near the windows, Penny, J.L., Abby, and Jessica waited, all of them watching Will and Cathy.

Cathy shoved Will's hand aside impatiently. "I can't talk to anyone right now. We can talk later."

"Excuse me." Will pushed his chair back and got up. "Sorry to take up your precious time. It won't happen again." He turned and made a thumbs-down gesture across the room. There was no way to explain her refusing to speak to them. Jessica was happy to fill up the silence with details of every phrase Danny Burns had uttered the day before.

Cathy's brain finally clicked. Suddenly Jennifer's explanations became clear. Cathy hastily scribbled a page of notes, overcome with relief. She shut her eyes and repeated the notes to herself, and miraculously, they made some sense.

With a jolt, Cathy realized the period bell had already rung. She piled her books together and made a dash for her next class.

11 ★

"Will, wait! I can hardly keep up with you."

"Then don't." Will stopped short and Cathy bumped into him.

"How about a hug? I think I passed my chemistry test, thanks to Jennifer." Cathy smiled proudly and stood waiting for a hug.

"Great. So now you have time for your old friends again. Thank you, Miss Rosen."

"What's with the sarcasm? Come on, Will. I'm sorry I couldn't talk at lunch."

"You must have been worried, to forget all about the Zodiacs and me yesterday."

Cathy stared at the ground, then laughed nervously. "I'm really sorry, Will. I meant to call and explain that I couldn't make it. I just got involved."

"Too involved to call me or anyone else and say you weren't going to show?" Will started to walk off alone.

"Wait. Let me tell you what happened." Cathy hurried again to walk beside Will. "Jen and I had a terrific idea for an article about the lost child. I haven't told anyone but you—I'm going right to the *Chronicle* to spring it on our editor."

"Hey, I'm real glad for you. Too bad you don't have time for ordinary folk like me anymore. I guess I'm pretty boring next to your big newspaper career."

"Come on, Will. Saturday I had an assignment. I had to go to Willburn. Everyone from the *Chronicle* did."

"Everyone?" Will snorted. "I happen to know Danny Burns wasn't there. Believe it or not, he seemed to think Starscope was pretty interesting."

"I can't worry about Danny Burns," Cathy said impatiently. "My story is great. An exclusive. Jennifer thinks we may have a shot at the front page."

"Hooray for Jennifer. What about your old friends? All you can talk about is your private-school pal."

"Give me a break." Cathy made her voice calm and level, as if talking to an angry child. "You know you always have a set notion of how things are going to work out, Will. It's the Taurus in you, but I don't mind and—"

"Don't throw horoscope in my face. You don't even care about it. I don't get you, Cathy. You should have been at the mall. Danny Burns—"

Cathy interrupted. "It's his bad luck that he wasn't covering this story. Don't ask me to feel sorry for him. Just think what a lucky break this is for me."

Will looked at her sharply. "This is a new attitude for you. Your friends used to be important. Is this Jennifer's influence too?"

"Be fair."

A car horn honked and Cathy looked in its direction. "Look, there's Jen. I've got to go. Call me later. And don't be so silly."

Cathy leapt into the front seat with Jennifer.

"How did the chem test go?" Jennifer asked eagerly.

"Jen—I nearly died." Cathy sank into the seat. "Panic attack. Then I pulled myself together and I'm pretty sure I did okay. Thanks to you."

"Great! We're lucky I've already had chem. You'll keep ahead of your class for the rest of the term."

"Imagine! Me, doing the best in a chem course. Unbelievable."

Jennifer gestured back toward the high school. "How's Will?"

"If you ask me, he's jealous of my new interests."

"Am I causing trouble?" Jennifer was instantly concerned.

"Don't worry," Cathy reassured her. "It's Starscope. But when I have a story in the *Chronicle* this week, everyone will forget this weekend."

"I hope you're right." Jennifer couldn't hide her own excitement. "Both our names across the top of the column under a big bold headline. 'A SHARED ORDEAL'—how do you like that? It gives an idea what the story is about, doesn't it?"

"Yeah—but editors write headlines, not interns."

"We can afford to give them that crumb of recognition," Jennifer teased.

Cathy crossed her legs, assuming a haughty pose. "Of course, the Pulitzer prize will be ours alone!"

Jennifer parked the car and she and Cathy hurried into the *Chronicle* building.

"Long time no see," Danny said brightly as they sat down.

Jennifer gave him a scathing look and Cathy was silent. They waited for Mrs. Mead, who came in late, apologizing to her staff.

As Charlie Ahearn predicted, the lost-child story was running on an inside page. For a moment, Cathy had her doubts about their story, but Jennifer gave her a reassuring wink and her spirits rose quickly.

"Wait—Mrs. Mead!" Jennifer and Cathy sprang from their chairs.

"I know it isn't usual procedure, but Cathy and I worked up an article about the search for the lost child."

"A behind-the-scenes human-interest angle," Cathy said. She took out the final draft of their story. "Mr. Ahearn gave us the go-ahead," she added.

Danny Burns stepped up to them. "I don't mean to start a trend, but I've written a proposal for a short piece myself." He handed the editor a few typed pages.

Jennifer was startled—she and Cathy exchanged surprised looks. What could Danny have found to write about over the weekend? Surely it wasn't anything as exciting as their story.

"Give me a few minutes to go through these. I'll call you when I'm ready," Mrs. Mead said.

"Did we goof? Was this a big mistake?" Cathy whispered anxiously as they waited outside.

"I don't know." Jennifer looked worried.

Danny had taken a seat at a desk far away from them. He wouldn't talk about his article.

"What could it be?" Cathy chewed on a pencil. "He looks so calm."

"He does play tennis every weekend," Jennifer said. "Maybe he wrote up a match."

"I wish he wouldn't look so cheerful."

"That's his strategy—keep the other guy worried."

"It works."

Finally Mrs. Mead called them into her office. She read silently through their articles one last time.

"Far be it from me to discourage eager young reporters," she said. "You know the usual procedures—your editor assigns your story after I approve it."

Jennifer felt doom approaching. Mrs. Mead didn't seem thrilled with them at all.

"There are exceptions. A scoop—an event no one else knows about yet. Perhaps an exclusive interview that falls into your lap."

Cathy felt suddenly ill. They wouldn't use the story— she was sure of it.

Mrs. Mead almost cracked a smile. "I admire initiative. And I must compliment both you girls. Your idea for the structure is excellent. Your instincts for the story behind the news are right on target. For this type of article, you have a wonderful grasp of the style required."

That was high praise, coming from Mrs. Mead.

"Thank you," Jennifer began. "We wanted to get the atmosphere of waiting—"

Mrs. Mead held up a hand to silence her. "I know you're eager to get something into print. You managed to work together and come out with one voice—very difficult. And you're still friends, I can see."

The girls laughed.

"But I can't use this. It's not being personal. Any editor would jump at the chance for a piece like this."

"Then why?" Cathy cried.

"It's space, isn't it?" Jennifer said curtly.

"But you could save it for next week," Cathy cried eagerly.

Mrs. Mead's eyes softened. "No one reads yesterday's news," she said kindly.

"But why?" Cathy said, choking on the words.

"Technicalities." Mrs. Mead pursed her lips. "Patrolman Nivins is the first problem. He assumed it was for your school newspaper. He didn't request clearance from his chief, and I know now that clearance will be denied."

"But he loved being interviewed," Cathy said. "Why couldn't he get clearance?"

"Whatever the reasons, the answer is no. It happens on bigger papers, Cathy, with bigger stories and bigger reporters. It's hard to swallow, but there you are."

"We could do something. Talk to them—I'll go over there."

"Me too," Jennifer said. "We'll get permission, I'm sure."

"There'll be other stories and we may need the chief's goodwill someday. Leave him out of it—understood?"

Cathy glanced at Jennifer. "I understand. But maybe you could still use Jennifer's part of the story. Did the mother grant her permission?"

"I don't mind if you can't," Jennifer said quickly. "These things happen."

"I'm glad you understand. Because the mother doesn't want any more publicity. She's had enough. She wants their lives back to normal. Sorry—but this time we can't go with it. Bad luck."

"All our hard work."

"I can't believe it."

"I am sorry, but it's my decision."

Cathy didn't bother hiding her disappointment.

"It hurts, I know." Mrs. Mead looked at the girls kindly. "It means a lot to you, I can see that."

"Something like this happened on our school paper."

Jennifer poked Cathy for her attention.

"What happened?" Cathy asked dutifully.

"It came down to the editor—run the story and lose sports equipment and scholarship money. The board was serious. The editors didn't run it."

"That's blackmail," Cathy cried.

"They fought about it. I guess the editor did what he thought was best. Can you imagine if the football team blamed him for not having uniforms and equipment, though?"

"Maybe he did the right thing," Cathy said grudgingly. "It's a tough choice."

"An editor's choice," Mrs. Mead said. "But we'll make it up to you."

"I guess deep down we knew this might happen," Jennifer said. "But it was a good first try, wasn't it?"

"It was." Mrs. Mead pointed her glasses at them. "Don't stop trying. You have talent, both of you."

She turned to Danny. He looked crestfallen. Mrs. Mead hadn't even mentioned his article yet.

"Now, this 'Operation Starscope' is something else," Mrs. Mead announced, adjusting her glasses.

Cathy gasped out loud, and Jennifer bolted upright in her chair.

"You're lucky, Mr. Burns." Mrs. Mead peered at him over the rim of her glasses. "Or else clairvoyant. Did you know the Collingwood Mall is putting out a special tabloid section in two weeks?"

"No." Danny looked stunned.

"Then it's luck. All the merchants have taken out ads, and we'll run stories about some of the stores. This Starscope promotion is just the kind of thing we can use. This Zodiac Club is a marvelous tie-in: people love to read good stories about teenagers. It's a good idea at the perfect time."

Cathy's disbelief grew as she listened. She glanced at

Jennifer, putting a finger to her lips, trying to warn her—
"Don't say a word about the Zodiacs," she wanted to scream.
How would it look that Cathy hadn't thought of the story
herself? What kind of instincts would Mrs. Mead think she
had now? None—for sure. Instead, she had ended up with
all her friends mad at her. Danny Burns would be a hero
to the Zodiacs.

"You can flesh out these notes. Find out about these
Zodiac girls. Are any of their parents active in the community? I'll send a photographer to the mall with you. Get
the story in by next Monday's deadline."

Danny's face looked like it might crack in half, his smile
was so wide.

"Is that all, Mrs. Mead?" Jennifer's voice shook only
slightly. Cathy was afraid to speak.

"That's all." Mrs. Mead began reading through a pile of
papers on her desk. Jennifer walked quickly from the room,
followed by a swaggering Danny Burns.

Cathy felt sick. She pulled herself heavily from the chair.
Somehow she got out of the office and ran down the long
hall to the ladies' room. She collapsed onto the couch and
lay motionless, staring at the ceiling.

"That was a rotten trick, Danny Burns." Jennifer was
seething with anger.

Danny looked up from the desk—he had already begun
reworking his Starscope article. He was grinning from ear
to ear.

"What? Come on, Jen. You would have done it to me.
By the way, tough luck on your little-lost-girl story."

Jennifer suppressed an urge to hit him. There were people
around. Instead she held on to a chair and lowered her voice
to a deadly hiss.

"You know I wouldn't have been this mean. I had a

chance at a good story—but I didn't go out of my way to humiliate anyone."

"So your friend Cathy is a little embarrassed. Is that it? Sorry—it couldn't be helped. She should have gotten the Starscope story herself."

"That's the trouble with you, Burns. You don't care who you hurt. Fair play means nothing to you."

"Cut it, Jen." Danny looked around uneasily. "Someone might hear you."

"Let them hear. Look, it's not your fault my story was killed. And you weren't wrong to think of the Starscope story. But the *way* you did it. Cathy never did anything to you." She bit her lower lip, startled to feel tears forming. She would never let Danny see her cry. She forced herself to get control before speaking again. At least Danny had stopped smiling. But he looked more puzzled than sorry.

"Don't you get it?" she said angrily. "You made Cathy look like a fool. What's she going to say when Mrs. Mead finds out she's a Zodiac? You should have warned her."

"I didn't do anything wrong," Danny insisted. "I saw a good story—same as you. Okay, I admit I knew Cathy would kick herself when she found out. And don't tell me you didn't gloat when you found out I didn't know about the lost kid. I'll bet you loved it."

"But I don't want to run my life that way anymore. I don't want to be rivals."

"Then why do I know you'll always try to beat me?" Danny thrust his head close to Jennifer's. "Every science fair of my life, you've been there to win first prize. Every exam I take, I see you getting all the answers right. The only thing you can't do as well as me is play tennis. You're everywhere, Jen. How do you think that makes me feel?"

"I haven't tried to hurt you." A tear escaped from Jennifer's eye. Furious, she wiped it away. She hated crying in front of him—she felt so weak.

Danny turned away.

"You're wrong, Danny. I have to do well. My parents expect it. *I* expect it. It has nothing to do with you."

"Oh no? I'm just supposed to be second best. Then we can go around together, and you'll have all the glory while I tag along behind. That's what you want—an adoring slave."

Jennifer stared at him, tears forgotten. "That's it—that's why we broke up. You think I was trying to shame you. You think I want someone weaker than I am. You're wrong, Danny. I really wanted you." The admission was too much for her. She was really crying now.

"Jen..." Danny reached out to her, the smug expression gone completely. He swallowed hard, and for a moment there was pain in his eyes.

Jennifer pulled away, hiding her face.

She thought of it suddenly—the big school dance they went to together. She remembered the look on his face when she came down the front stairs.

His words literally died on his lips when he looked up. It was just as Jennifer had planned.

Her mother had lent Jennifer her elaborately embroidered Chinese shoes, one of her prized possessions. Now the shoes fit perfectly. She felt like a princess, and the look in Danny's eyes told her she looked like one and that he wanted only to be her prince.

"Come on," her sister ordered. "If I'm driving you, we'd better get going. But if the two of you don't stop gawking at each other, I may be sick," her sister complained.

There was a spark of romance in her sister's soul after all. She pulled the car over several blocks away from the Academy.

"We're not there yet," Jennifer had said.

"It's a warm night. Why don't you walk the rest of the way?"

"Now, why did she do that?" Jennifer wondered out loud.

"Maybe so we'd have time to do this," Danny answered. Then he took Jennifer into his arms. "Jen," he whispered, staring intently into her dark eyes. He kissed her lightly on the mouth, held her away from him, and shook his head in wonder.

"I never knew you were so beautiful," he finally said, before pulling her close again for a long, wonderful kiss.

"We have to go in," Jennifer finally said, pushing Danny gently away from her.

"We'll pick up where we left off," Danny whispered.

Jennifer drifted into the ballroom in a happy daze.

"At last," Helen Dubin said, grabbing Jennifer's arm. "We couldn't imagine where you were."

Jennifer gave Helen a puzzled glance. Then the Academy headmaster called for silence and cleared his voice at the microphone.

"Ladies and gentlemen," he proclaimed, "it is always my pleasure to announce awards for academic achievement and excellence. But tonight we have a special honor to bestow." Someone handed him a small box.

Danny and Jennifer were frozen. All other academic prizes had been handed out earlier. Only the Westminster Science Award, which was a national award with a sizable scholarship attached to it, hadn't been designated yet. Both Danny and Jennifer had applied.

"Jennifer Chow," Mrs. Pressman boomed out, "come up here and accept this medal on behalf of yourself and the Academy."

Jennifer's heart leapt. She turned immediately to Danny, who still had one arm loosely around her waist. She hugged and kissed him joyously. But now she remembered he hadn't kissed her back. She hurried up to the podium to accept her award. The rest of that evening passed in a flurry.

When it was over, dazzled and flushed with excitement,

Jennifer sought out Danny, who was dancing with Suzanne Norton. She could smell smuggled beer on his breath. It bothered her that she would taste the beer when they kissed later, but it turned out she needn't have worried.

"It's been a big night," Danny said.

Outside, Jennifer gazed unhappily at the street. Her father was already parked at the curb.

"I guess we can't continue where we left off," Jennifer murmured. She was in a different mood now—excited and eager to show off her medal to her family. They would be so proud.

"Danny, I'm sorry you—"

"Hey, congratulations again," he said, kissing her lightly on the cheek.

"Danny, come to my house," she urged as they neared the car. "We can be alone later."

"I'd like to," he said, "but I'm not feeling so great. Probably all the beer I drank. I'll just go home."

She called him the next day, and the next, but he was always out playing tennis or doing chores. They went out casually a few times over the next weeks, but finally stopped.

Jennifer felt a stab of longing. He was still everything she wanted in a boy—but not if he wanted her to be less than she was. She couldn't cheat herself just to please him.

Her reverie was broken as Danny snapped his fingers under her nose. "Earth to Jennifer," he said.

"Do what you want," she said. "I don't care anymore. Write your crummy story."

She fled into the ladies' room. Behind her, Danny sat frozen at the desk, his eyes narrow and hard. Someone walking by knocked into his desk and said "Sorry" as he passed. The word startled Danny. It was the one word he wanted Jennifer to say. But she never would.

He inserted a sheet of paper into the typewriter in front

of him and began to type up his Starscope notes.

"May the best journalist win," he said out loud to no one at all.

"Shove over," Jennifer said to Cathy who was sitting at one end of the brown leather couch.

"You don't look so good. Have you been crying? We set ourselves up for a big fall. We shouldn't have expected so much. At least Mrs. Mead praised our work," Cathy said.

"You've changed your tune," said Jennifer.

"I've had time to think about it," Cathy explained. "Mostly I'm upset that I got everyone mad at me for nothing. If only I could make it up to everyone—and to myself. Maybe there's another terrific story to write."

Jennifer smiled bleakly.

"How do I explain that I snubbed everyone for a big story, when now there isn't any story at all? I think I just ruined my life."

"I'm sorry, Cath. I thought things would be different too."

"Hey, I don't blame you." Cathy shook Jennifer's arm. "I got myself into this mess. I made my choices."

"Me too, I guess." Jennifer collapsed limply against the wall.

"What do you mean?"

"It's a long story. It starts with a confession."

"Like what?"

Jennifer sighed. "Danny Burns means more to me than I let on. It's my fault we broke up." Jennifer told her the story.

"You couldn't help winning the award."

"If I had included Danny, he might have been with me that night. But I was so excited, I forgot about him. Danny thinks I only want to be superior to any boy. But I don't.

Why can't he admire me, even if sometimes I *am* smarter than he is?"

"That's tough," Cathy sympathized. "Some boys still think they have to be better than girls at everything. What are you going to do?"

Jennifer raised her eyebrows in surprise. "Do? I can't do anything. He's going to go on competing with me, and I'm going to go on competing with him."

Jennifer got up and angrily yanked a tissue from the dispenser. "Forget it, Cath. Some things aren't worth crying about."

"Are you sure about that?"

"Absolutely." But Jennifer kept her eyes turned away.

12 ★

Taurus does not like familiar patterns to change. You will cling to established routines, sometimes without considering that a change could be made for the better. Friends, family, and mate may find it difficult to live by the set rules you have determined. Since Taurus has a habit of hiding innermost feelings, friends and partners can become confused about your true emotions. Warning: others may be surprised to learn that practical, stubborn Taurus is a romantic at heart.

Jennifer turned a page, so absorbed in the newly purchased horoscope book that she didn't hear her mother enter her bedroom.

"I brought you tea and honey," her mother said.

"Mom, I didn't even hear you come in," Jennifer started guiltily.

"What's that book?" Mrs. Chow bent curiously to hold back a page of the horoscope book.

Jennifer flushed. "It's about the zodiac," she mumbled.

Her mother frowned. "I'm surprised at you, wasting your time with that. Don't you have schoolwork to do?"

"There's more to life than schoolwork," Jennifer snapped.

"Silly superstition won't help you."

"It isn't superstition," Jennifer insisted. "Read this Taurus description—it's really me."

"I doubt that. I can't see how anyone with a good scientific mind like yours can bother with such junk."

"Maybe I'm tired of scientific stuff."

"Rest a minute—then study."

"I don't believe it. Now you're trying to tell me when I can or can't relax. Did it ever occur to you I have my limits? I can't just think of work all the time. I've got to be able to be a normal kid once in a while."

"Wasting time with useless things won't help you get into the best college."

"I don't know if I care anymore. What good will it do me to go to a good school if I'm a social misfit the rest of my life?"

"Don't be ridiculous—you're nothing of the kind. You have lots of friends."

"I don't. I don't have the kind of friends I really want. I want to have fun, be free. I can't take this constant pressure. Let my sister be the scientist. I'm not sure I can cut it as a brain."

Jennifer grabbed her jacket from her bed where she had thrown it earlier. She pushed past her mother and ran down the stairs.

"Jen, where are you going?"

"Out," Jennifer called over her shoulder. "Just out."

A few minutes later she was ringing the bell to Cathy's house.

"Is Cathy in?" she asked Jane.

"Upstairs."

Jennifer paused outside Cathy's door, then knocked.

"Now what?" Cathy called irritably from inside.

"It's me—the *Chronicle*'s unknown reporter." Jennifer poked her head inside the door. "Can I come in?"

Cathy looked up in surprise. She was sitting at her desk, papers and pencils spread out in front of her.

"Sorry to come in like this."

"Forget it." Cathy swung her chair around. "I've been staring at the walls, daydreaming revenge. I can't believe everyone knew about Danny's article and no one told me."

"I'd believe anything now."

"How come you're here? I thought you had work to do."

"I had a stupid fight with my mother. She saw me reading a horoscope book and flipped out. It's not even her fault. I don't know why I'm in such a lousy mood."

"I've seen you looking better. Did you tell your parents our article was killed?"

"I told them. They were sympathetic and understanding. Maybe it's that—maybe it's something else."

"Like Danny Burns?"

Jennifer flung herself back onto Cathy's bed. "Is it that obvious?" She pulled the pillow over her face and Cathy laughed.

"It's nothing to be embarrassed about. He's not the worst guy in the world."

"He is for me," Jennifer moaned. "We're both too stubborn, too alike. Read your horoscope book. Neither one of us can say we're sorry and forget the past. I just want to get over him..."

"Why don't you just admit you like him and tell him?"

"It won't make any difference. He won't change. And we'd be right back to fighting."

"But you could kiss and make up afterward."

"That's true," Jennifer admitted with a sly smile. "But Mr. Burns would have to kiss back."

"Give him half a chance."

"I'll think about it."

"I did okay with Will."

"If only he'd give me some sign he was interested again—I could do it."

"Don't let pride get in your way. You can make the first move this time."

"Not now. Maybe soon, but not now."

Cathy couldn't help wondering if the time would ever be right for Jennifer and Danny.

"Between me and Danny and Will, you have nothing but Taurus trouble," Jennifer sighed.

"Maybe it's worth it." Cathy grinned.

The doorbell rang.

"I'll get it!" Jane called.

Cathy walked to the head of the stairs. She heard a muffled voice that sounded familiar.

"Jane? Is that Will?" No answer. "Jen," she called into her room, "come on down. Will's here."

Jane was standing by the front door, a long white envelope in her hand.

Cathy and Jennifer clattered down the stairs.

"Where's Will?" Cathy looked around, puzzled. "That was him, wasn't it?"

"Sort of," Jane said. She handed Cathy the envelope. "I'm supposed to tell you this is an official summons from the Zodiacs."

Cathy opened the front door, knocking Jane aside. She could see Will hurrying away. Frowning, she shut the front door behind her.

"Watch it," Jane complained. "It's not my fault your boyfriend doesn't like you anymore."

Cathy snatched the letter from Jane's hand.

"Come on, Jen. Let's go in the den. Alone," she added, glancing at Jane.

"You and your dumb Zodiacs," Jane grumbled. "You think I care what your crazy friends are up to?" She flounced into the kitchen.

"What is it?" Jennifer eyed the letter suspiciously.

"Look." Cathy held up the paper, giggling. "They drew zodiac symbols across the top of the paper. Very official-looking."

"What's wrong?"

The smile faded quickly from Cathy's face as she read. She raised troubled eyes to Jennifer.

"I don't believe it."

"What is it?" Alarmed, Jennifer rushed to her side.

"They wouldn't do this to me. They couldn't."

Jennifer grabbed the paper away. "They want you to appear and explain your actions to the Zodiacs."

Cathy nodded sickly. "There's a special meeting—they'll vote . . ."

"Has this happened before?"

"We haven't been a club that long," Cathy said. Her voice was almost a whisper. "Nothing like this has ever happened between us all—and I have to be the first." She rubbed her forehead.

"The meeting's two days away," Jennifer read. "Will you go?"

"I have to."

"What'll they do if you don't?"

"I don't know." Cathy's voice rose. "They wouldn't kick me out. It's only a club."

"They won't do anything—they're just angry, scaring you."

"I'm worried, Jen. Real worried."

"I'll go with you."

"You can't. You're already in trouble with your mother..."

"I don't care. This is more important."

"You'll have to lie about where you're going—don't do it."

"I won't lie. I'll tell the truth."

"Jen—then she'll never like me!"

"Listen, Cathy, I was part of the reason you missed Starscope."

"It was my own choice."

"I helped convince you. I can explain to them—you're not disloyal. They're making a big mistake, their feelings are hurt."

Cathy didn't answer. Jennifer got up and paced the room.

"This burns me up," Jennifer said. "Are they the kind of friends who drop you the first time you make a mistake?"

"We've always stuck together before."

"Oh yeah?"

"It's true! I could name dozens of times... This is getting us nowhere."

"They should be more understanding," Jen said stubbornly.

"That attitude won't help," Cathy said wryly. "I think they're after an apology. I should have made it myself before."

"You have nothing to apologize for."

"Okay—so we'll tell my side of the story—no apologies."

"And don't take any criticism either."

"Jen, you're angrier than I am!"

"Maybe so. Maybe because they're the ones who have you for a friend all the time. And look how they treat you."

"You're jealous!"

"So what? If we convince them to take you back, I'll never see you."

"That's not true. There's the *Chronicle*."

"That's work. I guess...I want to be friends all the time. The Zodiacs will take up all your spare time."

"This is a mess." Cathy reread the letter. "I'm stuck. I can't lose my friends. I'm with them every day at school, I've known most of them all my life. But I want us to be friends too."

"I'd have to be a Zodiac to be your real friend," Jennifer said bitterly.

"Well, why not?" Cathy sprang up from her chair, grabbing Jennifer's shoulder and shaking her.

"Hey—cut it out!"

"Why not?" Cathy cried gleefully. "I'll propose you for a member. Then we can both be Zodiacs—both or nothing!"

"Then they'll really kick you out—fast! They don't want me."

"So we'll form our own club. Taurus-Leo only."

"Cathy, be serious. It's a dumb idea. Very dumb."

"Look, if we convince them to take me back, I'll propose you for membership too. I've decided."

"You're pushing your luck."

"Come on—say you'll let me do it. It'd be great."

"Maybe."

"A maybe from you is almost as good as a yes," Cathy cried happily.

"With me or not, I hope you get back in the club," Jennifer said. "I was stupid to be jealous—selfish."

"Forget it. You need a chance to have friends you can relax with. Everyone wants to have fun, Jen. You just need it more than the rest of us."

"No matter what happens to me, you've got to be a Zodiac again. I'll help."

"Okay. It's a deal. You help me—and I'll help you. With the Zodiacs and with Danny Burns."

"I never thought I had so many problems," Jennifer joked.

"We all do."

In school the next day, most of the Zodiacs stayed away from Cathy.

"Will, wait up!" she called to him at the end of the day.

He heard her but disappeared around a corner. Defeated, Cathy went on to her job without making up with anyone.

"I'm almost ready to give up," she told Jennifer as they sat together that afternoon. "I feel like I'm on trial and Will is one of the judges."

"It'll work out," Jennifer reassured her.

"I can't stand it. Abby won't talk to me—she's the one friend I thought would stick by me."

Jennifer nodded. "You always say how great she is."

"She was—once. Did I really commit a crime?"

"What about Will? Any luck with him?"

"He's still not talking...won't come near me. If only I knew what he was thinking. I can't work, I can't sleep—I keep seeing myself at the meeting with a noose around my neck..."

"Cathy!"

Cathy grinned. "Only kidding—but can you blame me?"

"Hey, maybe I can get Will to talk to you."

"I'd love it. It's awful to lose your friends *and* your boyfriend in one blow. I never realized how lonely I'd be without Will. I miss him."

"I think I can get him to listen to you."

"I doubt it. As soon as he sees me, he runs away."

"I know a place he can't run away from." Jennifer looked around the office to see who might hear. "I'll whisper, just in case."

"We can't! Jen—it's crazy. If we get caught, we're dead."

"Name another way," Jennifer challenged. "Just one."

"I can't let you take the risk. There must be another way."

"Come on—let me be a real friend," Jennifer insisted.

"I have a feeling a 'real friend' wouldn't let you get involved," Cathy muttered.

"You can't do it without me."

"Okay."

Jennifer hugged her.

"But you have to promise me—"

"What?"

"You'll let me get you and Danny back together."

"Wait a minute—that's not fair."

"It's that or nothing," Cathy said. "I know you two should get together again."

"How are you going to work this miracle?"

"I have no idea. But you're not the only one who can scheme."

"If tonight's plan works, I'll do it for you."

"And if it doesn't work?"

"Both of us will be in too much trouble to worry about it."

"All right. We'll give it a try."

The plan was simple. Cathy went to the library with Jennifer after work that night to study. She hardly felt guilty when she called her parents to explain: "Mom? We need to study late tonight, okay?"

"But, Cathy, the library closes soon."

"We'll go back to Jen's and then she'll drive me home."

"It's a school night, Cathy. Don't make it later than ten-thirty."

"Eleven? Please, Mom—that's not enough time."

"At the very latest. And I mean home by then. Understood?"

"I'll try."

Cathy hung up quickly.

"Not too bad," she told Jennifer. "We'll make it by eleven, won't we?"

"That's up to Will." Jennifer took a deep breath. "This is the only sneaky part. But it has to be done."

Jennifer dialed her house and repeated the same story to her mother—except Jennifer said they'd be studying at Cathy's house. She hung up the phone and crossed her fingers. "The rest is up to Will."

The library closed.

"It's too early to go to Will's," Cathy said. "And we can't go to either of our houses."

"Pick your favorite food," Jennifer said. "We'll wait until ten and then try Will's."

They spent an uneventful hour devouring chocolate-covered doughnuts.

"We need the sugar for energy," Jennifer insisted.

"We need the sugar like a hole in the head," Cathy answered. "And we may have one—going through with this scheme."

"We can call it off."

"No, now that we've come this far, let's see it through. But I'm nervous," Cathy admitted.

"I know. But it's going to work. Besides—it's kind of fun," Jen said.

"Where's the straightlaced serious student I used to know?" Cathy chastised her. "Let's go. Fast—I'm afraid someone's going to stop us any minute." She looked back over her shoulder.

"Creepy, huh?"

"I've been thinking. Until now I *did* take Will for granted. I felt safe. Even when I put him down I figured he was crazy about me and I didn't need to worry. Now I'm worried that he'll dump me."

"You'll find out soon," Jennifer said grimly.

They paid their bill and drove to Cathy and Will's neighborhood.

"Is that his house?" Jennifer asked.

Cathy nodded and Jennifer parked the car a few houses away from the Coffmans'. She turned off the motor and headlights. Then they waited.

"It's taking forever. Don't those people go to bed?"

"Wait—look." The downstairs lights went out. Cathy watched closely. "That's Will's room," she said, pointing to a corner window at the back of the house. The room was dark.

"He must be already asleep. Let's do it."

"Wait a few minutes," Cathy urged.

The minutes went by slowly. "It's eleven," Jen whispered nervously. "We've got to do it now. I'm so late already I'll get killed. Did you get the water pistol?"

Cathy whispered back, "Got it and loaded it. I feel stupid though."

"Give it to me. And wish me luck."

"Good luck." Cathy held up crossed fingers as Jennifer got out of the car and opened the hood. She ran lightly up to Will's dark bedroom window. She dug up a handful of pebbles and tossed them against the glass.

"Will," she called softly, tossing more pebbles. She was about to give up when Will's face appeared at the window—groggy and crumpled-looking. He shook his head a few times as if to clear it.

"Will—open the window." Jennifer gestured wildly.

Will's face disappeared, then came back with his glasses

in place. He raised the window cautiously. "What's going on?"

"It's Jennifer. I'm in big trouble—my car's stalled . . . out front. Come out, but don't wake anyone! I'm supposed to be home."

Jennifer waited nervously, glancing back at her parked car. Where was Will?

Finally she heard a door close softly, and Will appeared at the back door, a pair of jeans and a sweater thrown over his pajamas.

"Tell me again—what's happening?"

Jennifer babbled a stream of incoherent words.

Will followed her across the lawn to the car.

"This is it?" Will paused, glancing at the motor.

"That's it. Please help me. Try to start it," Jennifer urged. Her hand crept to the water pistol in her pocket—just in case—but Will had fallen for it.

He opened the front door.

The light flashed on and Cathy popped up on the front seat.

"Wha . . ."

"Don't shout—don't move," Cathy warned. She pulled him onto the seat behind the steering wheel. He stared at her, bewildered and suspicious. Jennifer stood guard at the door, the water pistol drawn and aimed at Will.

"I had to do it, Will. You wouldn't talk to me."

"Is this a kidnapping?"

"No. Just guaranteeing that you'll stay here awhile."

"What's with the water pistol?"

"Whiskey."

"Whiskey?"

Cathy had to stifle a laugh—it seemed so funny all of a sudden. She bit her lip.

"If you try to escape, we'll shoot whiskey at you and ring your doorbell. Your parents will wake up—you'll have to explain why you're up and reeking of alcohol."

"You're nuts." Will stared at Jennifer's carefully aimed water pistol. "Tell her to back off. I'll talk," he said dramatically.

Cathy waved Jennifer away from the car. Then she faced Will.

"This is serious, Will. I'm going nuts. Are you my friend"—her voice broke—"my boyfriend . . . or not?"

Will didn't answer.

"Then you want to break up—for good?"

Will turned his head away. Cathy grabbed one of his hands. She felt tears coming, although she tried to hide it from Will.

"I still need you. I'm sorry about everything."

"Cathy . . ." Will tried to pull his hand away. "Come on, stop this."

"I can't. I never meant to hurt you or anyone. I wanted to do something to impress you—make you all proud. Was that so terrible? Now, even my job is all screwed up. Everything's coming out all wrong."

Will put an arm around her. He struggled to remain cool. "Look, Cathy, don't cry. I don't know, it doesn't sound as bad when you tell it. You acted like my work and my ideas were unimportant. All you cared about was your own glory."

"That's not true! I got caught up . . . I wanted . . . I guess I wanted everything."

Will moved closer, folding his other arm around her. Cathy snuggled into his shoulder—it was wonderful to feel comforted again. Will hugged her tight. He kissed the top of her head and rubbed her back.

"Maybe it wasn't so terrible," he said.

"You think so?"

"You hurt me, but I guess you hurt yourself more."

"Don't let me go, Will."

"No way." He held her and kissed her on the mouth.

Jennifer walked farther away from the car to give them privacy.

Cathy pulled back from him. "So... are we all right again?"

"Yeah—we're all right. I never really wanted to break up. I was just angry. Everyone was. Is," he corrected.

Cathy groaned. "Oh no. Are they going to kick me out? It's not fair! I didn't do anything that terrible."

Will looked at her thoughtfully. "When you didn't show up, a lot of the excitement about Starscope just faded. Everyone felt betrayed."

"Even when Danny Burns came?" Cathy said. "I thought he perked up everyone's interest."

"His article is making a big difference. All the stores are signing up—they can't afford not to. Bad publicity."

"Where does that leave me, though?"

"Cathy, Danny can't replace you, no way. Would I kiss him like this?"

"I'm not sure."

Will grabbed her and she laughed breathlessly.

"Will," she said softly, "I still feel a little sorry for myself."

"So?"

She leaned toward him. "So I know the perfect way to cheer me up."

There was a sharp rapping on the windshield—Jennifer's water pistol. She opened Will's door. "Hey, we're running out of time. Break it up."

"It's almost midnight!" Cathy looked up in alarm. "We've got to get home."

Will started to get out of the car. Cathy touched his arm.

"Will . . . if you can, talk to the others."

He kissed her lightly. "I'll try."

"Can you make it back inside okay?" Jennifer asked him.

"If I don't, I'll tell my folks two beautiful females tried to kidnap me. They'll understand."

Cathy insisted they wait until Will signaled from his bedroom. Then Jennifer started the car and they drove away.

"Did I feel stupid," Jennifer complained good-naturedly. "Standing there with a loaded water pistol. . . . Will didn't need much threatening, did he?"

Cathy blushed. "I'll be happy to do the same for you."

Jennifer glanced at her. "If only it were that easy. Just appear at midnight—and voilà! Instant passion."

"Don't worry, we'll get you and Danny back together."

"Right now I'm more worried about getting back in my house."

They reached the end of Cathy's block.

"Don't wait," Cathy insisted. "You go on home. I'll be fine."

"If you're sure . . ."

"I'm worried about you now."

"Me too. If it were this easy to get away all the time, we could have a whole secret life. 'Students by day, adventurers by night.'"

"Get out of here," Cathy commanded.

"Can't take the threat of danger?" Jennifer teased.

"Go!" Cathy called, shutting the car door behind her.

As Cathy ran for the safety of her back door, her fear returned. She edged the kitchen door open soundlessly. She was almost safe now—the house was silent. Everyone had gone to sleep and she might make it upstairs without waking them. The thought of Will's kiss warmed her—at least part of her life felt back in place. She still had Will. She could survive. She could face the Zodiacs.

Gratefully she ran up the stairs to her room. Halfway

there, Jane's door opened. Cathy immediately stretched her arms in an exaggerated yawn, climbing the rest of the stairs.

"Jane!" she called softly. "What are you doing up?"

"I thought I heard a noise. Was it you?"

"Sorry, I was downstairs. Thirsty."

Jane walked closer to Cathy, leaning over the top of the railing and blocking the stairs. She nodded knowingly. "Dry throat?"

"Right." Cathy gave her a sleepy smile.

"Made yourself some warm milk?"

"Right again."

"Weren't you supposed to be home hours ago?"

Cathy stiffened. "Were you spying on me? You should be asleep."

Jane's eyes opened in innocent surprise. "Spying? I was *worried.*"

"Okay, I got home a little late. Then I went outside. For fresh air."

"Isn't it funny that Jennifer was driving by . . . for fresh air, I suppose. At midnight."

"You little sneak."

"I saw it all," Jane said smugly.

"If you tell . . ."

"What?"

Cathy immediately changed her tone of voice. It was no good threatening Jane.

"It was an emergency. We had to talk."

"Ever hear of telephones?"

"Look . . . nothing bad happened—"

Jane stifled a yawn, interrupting her. "I'm tired. Here's the deal—I won't tell, if you promise to cover for me sometime. Okay?"

"Do I have a choice?"

Jane smiled. "Sleep well."

"You too."

Jane paused. "You wouldn't tell what you did if I . . ."

"No way. We made our deal."

Their mother's voice suddenly called from her room: "Girls! Cathy—is that you?"

"Sorry, Mom," Cathy called.

"Are you just getting in? It's very late."

Cathy gave Jane a warning look. "No, I've been down in the kitchen. I wasn't sleepy."

"Well, get sleepy," their mother called firmly.

Jennifer parked the car up the street, close enough so it could be seen if anyone checked for it, but not so close she would wake her parents. She crept toward the kitchen door. A light was on upstairs in her bedroom—and in the kitchen. Her heart caught in her throat. Her father stood in the doorway. She snapped to attention; her blood drained completely away.

"Jennifer!" Her father's voice cracked, anger and fear mixing in his tone.

He flung open the kitchen door, and Jennifer stepped inside. Her mother stood a few feet away, blinking at her as if at a ghost.

"Thank God," her mother cried. "I knew she was all right."

"*Are* you all right?" her father demanded.

Jennifer nodded weakly. Her mind struggled to function. She felt like a trapped spy in an old war movie. The pressure was awful. She licked her lips, praying for time.

"I had this terrible feeling," her mother was saying. "I woke up knowing something was wrong. I looked in on you, I always do . . ."

"You do?" Jennifer said faintly.

"I was calling the police," her father said. "You caught me just in time. Where were you?"

"I . . ."

"Don't tell me you were at Cathy's. We called at eleven, and she wasn't home either."

"I know. We got hungry and went out for a snack."

"At that hour? The Rosens let her?"

"We went much earlier," Jennifer said. The lies surprised her—they seemed to invent themselves. "But we got talking and lost track of the time—sorry. I took Cathy back home, then I got all the way back here and realized I'd forgotten some books. I was so worried about them, I drove all the way back to Cathy's again. I know it's late, I'm really sorry."

"Worried? You had work to do, didn't you?" her mother said. "I told you—you can't spend so much time with these new friends of yours. You'll fall behind."

"You were right," Jennifer agreed hastily. "I *was* behind." Was she getting herself in deeper and deeper?

"Where are they?" her father asked.

She stared at him blankly.

"The books you left at Cathy's."

Jennifer was holding two notebooks. "They weren't there," she stuttered. "I must have left them at the library after all. I'll...have to go back tomorrow night to get them." She realized she had just given herself the perfect alibi for the Zodiac meeting. The lies were building.

"Crazy kids," her father muttered. But there was relief in his voice.

"She's under pressure," her mother said. "Maybe she can't handle the *Chronicle* job too...."

"No," Jennifer insisted. "I can do it—please, I'll be more careful with my time from now on."

"All right—but...go on to bed. You'll do well."

"Thanks, Mom. I will."

13

Cathy could hardly wait to see Will. She hurried across the school's front lawn. Abby, J.L., Penny, and Jessica were standing near the trees. Cathy skirted around the yard and went in the opposite direction. Will was out back, tossing a football around with a group of boys. She caught his eye and he passed the football and headed for her. Cathy waited, leaning against the rough bricks of the building, trying to seem casual.

"Hey." Will leaned over her, stretching one arm straight out to lean on so that she was shaded by him—protected.

"Hi, you."

"Don't smile so wide," he said, smiling widely himself. "You'll give us away."

"I know. We're not supposed to be 'friends' again, are we?"

"Nope."

"I saw them all out front."

"What's the matter? Not into confrontations today?"

"No way. If they want to talk to me before the meeting—okay. But I'm not starting any conversations."

"I'll help, if I can. I see J.L. first period. I'll put in a good word for you."

"J.L.!" Cathy rolled her eyes. "She's really out to get me."

"You left her party rather rudely."

"Now we're back where we started—I had something else to do! Everyone misses parties sometimes . . . and meetings."

"But not *the* project," Will said. "They have a point."

Cathy sighed. "Let's not talk about it. How was J.L.'s party anyway? No one told me a thing."

"Well, Danny Burns was the hit. He beat me at telling jokes."

Cathy laughed. "Did he impress everybody?"

Will shook his head. "You know, Danny gets away with murder. I don't know how he got me started. At first it seemed really friendly, and then he took it so seriously I realized he wanted to beat me! But Danny is a hard guy to turn down. There's something about him..."

"You like him though, don't you?" Cathy asked.

"Hard not to. He's really a good guy."

"How come," Cathy said, feeling her way slowly, "when you and Danny become friends, no one resents it?"

"What do you mean?"

"I feel like people resent my new interests. My job, maybe even Jennifer. I bet I could've missed Starscope for some other reasons, and it wouldn't be a big deal at all."

"But you chose to miss it."

"What if I chose to miss it again? Or miss a meeting anyway—is that so terrible? What's the point of a club if it turns into a chore?"

"Maybe that's what you should tell your friends."

"Do you really think that?"

"Saved by the bell."

The bell had rung and Cathy slipped out from under Will's arm.

"No answer—no kiss."

She twisted away, but Will bent and caught her with a quick kiss.

"Hey," she protested. But she didn't move away and her eyes weren't the least bit angry.

"Oops—sorry." Will bent over her again. "Here, I'll take it back." He kissed her again and walked off quickly.

Cathy took a deep breath and ran into the building. One way or another, she would get through this day.

* * *

Jessica banged with her fist against the tabletop. Cathy sat to her right, perched on an uncomfortable wooden chair. The others were arranged around the big wooden table in Jessica's basement, all except Jennifer, who sat on the old couch against the wall—an "unofficial observer," as Jessica had dubbed her. Jennifer was allowed to watch but not to comment.

"I'd like to read a document—a statement, actually," Jessica began. "It explains how we all feel." She cleared her throat. "'I, Cathy Rosen, confess to conduct unbecoming a Zodiac member. Namely, I did willfully obstruct the natural completion of Project Starscope by neglecting to appear at the aforesaid project on—'"

"Whoa!" Cathy cried. "What's this?"

"Where'd you get that legal junk?" J.L. marveled.

"Hold everything," Abby protested. "This isn't a trial. No one has to confess."

"And who put you in charge, Jessica?" Mara folded her arms stubbornly.

"I *took* charge. Someone had to, if we want this thing to run right," Jessica insisted.

"What 'thing'? We're going to talk a few things over, that's all."

"Wait, Abby," Penny protested. "I agree with Jess. I mean, we don't need to act like a lynch mob, but Cathy—"

"—was seriously wrong," Jessica finished smugly. "I think we all agree to that."

"No we don't," Cathy said.

"Look, we all agree we felt let down," Abby said. "But she didn't commit a crime."

"She didn't do her share of the work," J.L. said. "We all had other things to do—"

"But she did have to consider her job," Abby answered. "She couldn't risk losing it." Abby's eyes met Cathy's and

Cathy nodded her thanks. "It could happen to any of us. Sometimes you have to choose."

"I really resent this. Cathy's not the only one with choices," Penny cried. "We all chose to keep our promise to be there."

"That's not the point, Penny," Cathy said.

"What is the point?"

"That friendship isn't easy," Elizabeth suggested.

"No," J.L. said. "The point is not to use your friends."

"I didn't use anybody," Cathy protested.

"But you expect to 'drop in' when it's convenient for you," J.L. said. "The Zodiacs can't work that way."

"That's not fair." Cathy repeated what she'd told Will earlier. "No one should be afraid to miss a meeting or some activity."

Elizabeth agreed. "We have to be able to miss meetings—if it's important."

"Who decides what's important?" Mara turned to Penny. "Suppose you had a date. Would you turn down a night out with Mr. Wonderful?"

"She would if we told her to," Jessica said.

"Wrong. We can't act like dictators."

Jessica gave up. "I'm confused. How do we know who's in the club, then?"

"Our friends," Elizabeth said simply.

"But a friend would be there," Jessica countered.

"I made arrangements for Starscope." Mara bent eagerly over the table. "I had to cancel a piano lesson."

"You hate piano lessons."

"Wait a minute!" Elizabeth jumped to her feet. "We sound like a bunch of backbiting creeps! What's happening here?"

"I'll tell you what's happening," Jennifer said quietly, but with authority, from the couch.

"Out of order," Jessica said immediately, banging her imaginary gavel.

"Jess," Cathy warned, "don't push your luck."

"Let her talk," J.L. said. "This *is* getting out of hand."

"She's not a Zodiac," Jessica protested lamely.

Jennifer walked to the table, standing between Jessica and Cathy. Her dark eyes blazed, but her voice was soft and controlled.

"I'll tell you what's happening. You've put friendship on trial—as if there's a right or wrong to it. You're all forgetting one detail. In a way, you all let Cathy down."

"What?" Jessica cried.

"That's right. You haven't given her a chance to explain her side of it. What kind of friendship is that?"

"I *did* feel let down—no one told me about Danny Burns's big story," Cathy said. "You owed me that. Someone should have told me—not let me find out at the newspaper meeting. It was humiliating, I felt like a fool. I couldn't admit I was a Zodiac after that. So you've already paid me back. And that's not the basis for friendships—revenge."

No one said anything.

"If it helps any," Jennifer said quietly, "I know Cathy felt awful about missing Starscope. She didn't want to. The editor pressured her, I pressured her—it's not the kind of chance you pass up. She thought you'd all understand."

"You don't know all the details," J.L. said. "And I resent that you came to my house for one minute, and dragged Cathy away with you."

"This is awful," Elizabeth cried. "I hate this! What if I have to miss a meeting, or someone's party, or a project— is this going to happen to me too? Or is it just because Cathy has a new interest, and we're jealous? I'm not in this club to be afraid—I didn't join to be told what to do. Doesn't anyone remember? We were 'Hill kids' and 'River kids'—practically sworn enemies, and for no reason at all! This club was for friendship—learning to accept each other. No one's said J.L. can't ride horses anymore, or Penny can't play tennis. We're all allowed to have other interests. The main thing was, we liked each other and wanted to have fun together. That's all."

"Hey," Abby said after a moment's silence. "Don't look so glum. We got carried away—I did, I don't know why. My feelings were hurt."

"Well, nobody's perfect," J.L. said gruffly.

"I was hoping someone would say that," Cathy joked, "eventually."

Jennifer cleared her throat. "I'm sorry I said anything. I just got upset..."

"I guess we did get carried away," Mara said softly.

"No one's asked Cathy if she still wants to be a Zodiac," Jessica said in a subdued voice.

"Of course I do," Cathy cried. "I always did. I'll just have to fit everything in."

"I'm not sure why I was so angry," Penny admitted. "I don't want you to quit the club anyway."

"Jen," Cathy said, "thanks for sticking up for me."

Jennifer shrugged uncomfortably. "I'm sorry, J.L.," she said, "I didn't mean to crash your party."

"Forget it," J.L. said quickly. "I didn't mean to sound like such a creep."

Cathy put her arm through Jessica's. "You haven't said anything, Jess. Still angry?"

Jessica looked away. "I guess not."

"Friends?"

Jessica pouted for a moment, then flashed her impish grin. "I can't stay mad at anyone," she said with a giggle.

"That's a relief!"

"I can't tell you how sick I was about this," Cathy said, and a flood of words poured out of her. Everyone began talking at once, apologizing or forgiving or explaining herself. Jennifer hung back, away from them, feeling very much an outsider.

"I can't wait for you to see how well Starscope is doing," Abby told Cathy. "You *can* come this weekend, can't you?"

"I hope so," Cathy answered. "I'd hate to go through this again!"

Everyone laughed but Mara, who sheepishly raised a hand to get their attention. "I had to promise to take two piano lessons to make up for last Saturday's."

"Don't worry," Cathy laughed. "I'll be there to replace you, Mara."

"Hey, Jennifer," Abby said, "why don't you come too?"

Suddenly Cathy realized Jennifer was standing alone. She grabbed her new friend's arm. "Can you, Jen? Just for an hour or two."

Jennifer couldn't hide her pleasure. "I'd really like to. I have so much studying . . ."

"If you can, come. If not, don't," Elizabeth said quickly. "No pressure, okay?"

"Terrific," Cathy cried. "Isn't it, Jess?"

"Yeah, that's great," Jessica answered. But her smile wavered. Would she get Danny Burns's attention with Jennifer around? Or didn't it matter?

"Hey—sorry, but I've got to leave," Jennifer said.

"Trouble with your parents?" Cathy asked. She and Jennifer had exchanged stories about the night before. Cathy felt terrible that Jennifer had lied to protect her.

"There will be, if I don't get back to the library."

"Then go—no more trouble, please," Cathy said.

"It's okay," Jennifer assured her. "I can get lots done tonight."

"See you tomorrow at the paper," Cathy said.

After she had gone, Cathy decided to tell the other girls what Jennifer had done to help her with Will.

"I like that girl a lot," Abby commented. "She has character."

"She does," Cathy agreed. "And she really thinks the Zodiacs are terrific."

"Yeah—after we nearly lynched you," J.L. said dryly.

"We can laugh about it now," Cathy assured her. "Jen doesn't know how great it is to have you guys on her side."

"You know," Abby said thoughtfully, "maybe we should ask Jennifer to join. At least we'd get a chance to prove we're not the horrible people she saw tonight."

Cathy's eyes sparkled. "I'm glad to hear you say that."

"Anybody object?" Abby asked. "We've never taken an outside member."

"All of us were 'outsiders' when this club started," Mara reminded her.

"Jen's a Taurus," Cathy pointed out. "We don't have a Taurus yet."

"Let's think about it, okay?"

"Absolutely." Cathy hugged Abby, then grew suddenly somber.

"What's the matter?"

"Jen's parents aren't crazy about her getting involved with lots of social activities. She really has it tough— studying all the time, pressure from her folks..."

"Maybe when they see Danny's article they'll know we're a worthwhile group," Mara said. "Ooops—sorry, Cath. Touchy subject."

"It's okay—I have to get used to the idea. Besides, let him write about the Zodiacs—I *am* a Zodiac!"

"This wasn't such a bad night after all," Elizabeth said. "We may have gained a member instead of losing one."

"We're the old Zodiacs again—all for one and one for all," Abby said.

"That's unanimous," Penny agreed with relief. "Now, did anyone think to bring refreshments?"

14

"What's up, Helen?" Cathy paused at the receptionist's desk.

It was the day after the Zodiac meeting and Cathy was late getting to the *Chronicle*.

"Either you did something really good or really bad. Mrs. Mead wants to see you in her office right away."

"It couldn't be anything too bad. I've been proofreading all week—did I mess up?"

"Jennifer's already in there," Helen said.

"Reading my mind again?"

"I've raised five girls, remember?"

"I remember." Cathy chuckled.

Cathy hurried to Mrs. Mead's office. Jennifer greeted her with a wide-eyed shrug as Cathy pulled a chair up to the editor's desk.

"Here's a special assignment for you two," she announced, pulling a sheaf of papers from a folder. "I'm giving you a chance to rewrite an article—for publication, not practice," she added as Cathy and Jennifer exchanged surprised glances.

"Since you have worked together before—and since Danny Burns is getting something into print—here's your chance."

She handed the pages to Cathy, who glanced at them briefly, then handed them on to a dumbfounded Jennifer.

"It's not as exciting as your missing-child story—but we need to run it."

"It's about converting unused warehouses into condominiums," Jennifer told Cathy. She turned to Mrs. Mead. "Why the rewrite?"

"It needs updating and it could stand better organization—something you seem quite good at. Double-check those construction costs—they could be higher by now. Have it ready by Monday's deadline."

As usual, Mrs. Mead dismissed them simply by plunging back into her work.

"At last! In print!"

"And I think she really likes our work," Jennifer said gleefully.

"She must," Cathy said. "I knew our story was good, Jen. This proves it."

"Well, it's not our own idea, like Danny's story—but it'll be printed!"

"Hey, I almost forgot!" Cathy pulled Jennifer aside. "I've got other great news for you."

"What? Tell me."

Neither of them noticed Danny Burns come out of the darkroom area behind them. Hearing their voices, he paused.

"The other girls agree—"

"What?" Jennifer urged.

"Well, we don't have a Taurus Zodiac member," Cathy teased.

"And? So?"

"So we thought you might help us out—be our Taurus."

"Seriously?" Jennifer's eyes lit up instantly.

"Seriously."

"They want me?"

"It's a good possibility."

Jennifer grabbed Cathy in a bear hug. "I'd love it! Oh, I would!"

Cathy forced herself to be stern. "I want you to consider carefully—remember, your parents..."

"I know," Jennifer said in dismay. "Another close call like the other night and I'm done for."

"Believe me, I'll understand if they won't let you join. Especially after our escapade—maybe you'd better lay low for a while."

Jennifer struck a carefree pose. "Oh? Should I be worried? I'll just tell my parents I stayed out at night to meet a boy. What's the big deal?"

"What's wrong with a little kissing by moonlight?" Cathy joined in.

"Or kidnapping a boy from his room?"

"Oh no!" Cathy suddenly gasped. "Jen, the whiskey! What'd you do with it?"

"That—I nearly died. It was in my pocket when my parents caught me sneaking in! I flushed it down the toilet."

Behind them, Danny stood, arms stiffly at his sides, hands strained into fists. He had heard enough. He turned abruptly and went back to the darkroom, where no one could see the pain and disbelief in his eyes.

"You're right, though," Jennifer said, sobering. "I do have to take it easy. Lying is not good—I hate it. I'll break this idea gently; let my parents get used to it."

"That'll be good," Cathy said. "Give everyone time to think the idea over."

"Meanwhile, we'd better start this article."

"Neither of us is going to miss Starscope this time," Cathy agreed.

Later that day Jennifer noticed Danny hanging around her. She decided to try and talk to him.

"Danny, guess what," she began. "We have an assignment." Jennifer thought her news would break the ice. Instead, Danny barely looked at her. His eyes wavered toward her for an instant, but then he turned and walked on.

"What's with him?" Cathy wondered. "The one time we're really happy, he's really down."

"I can't figure him out," Jennifer sighed.

The crowd around the Computer Capers store cheered as Will dramatically held a fishbowl stuffed with cash above his head.

"Starscope is a rousing success!" he announced.

Flashbulbs popped. "Hold it again." Will repeated the gesture while the photographer snapped another picture.

He reloaded his camera while Danny interviewed Will and Harlan.

Cathy huddled with Jennifer on the fringes of the crowd, shuddering each time a flash went off.

"Don't worry," Jennifer laughed. "He's not pointing the camera anywhere near you."

"I can't help it. I still don't want Mrs. Mead to know I'm a Zodiac."

"She won't care. She loved our condo rewrite. She even said we put some life into a pretty dull subject."

"Right. And I'm not going to blow my new image," Cathy said. "The thing is, are *you* ready to be a Zodiac?"

Jennifer glanced around uneasily. "Don't say that out loud—I have the creepy feeling my parents are behind us somewhere."

Cathy laughed. "I thought they were softening, not forbidding it anymore. At least, your mom isn't."

"No—it's more like she's convinced I've ruined my life."

"I guess they could tell how much it means to you."

"I guess."

"Anyway, there's nothing wrong with taking a break. You studied all morning."

Jennifer glanced at her watch. "And I should go back to the library soon."

"Not until you answer—Zodiac or not?"

"Yes, of course," Jennifer said. "I want to tell all the girls myself—thank them for asking me."

"Are you kidding? The way you handled Starscope today! You were a whiz—people were lining up to talk to you. You can really turn on the charm when you want to."

"Typical Taurus," Jennifer quipped. "Just like Danny."

"And Will," Cathy added. "It's true. Different as you all are, you've got that in common."

"That's *all* Danny and I have in common—we don't talk at all anymore."

"Don't worry—I owe you, remember? One boyfriend, all kissed and made-up. I haven't forgotten."

"I think it's hopeless," Jennifer said. "Better work on my mom instead—convince her the Zodiacs will enrich my life or get me into the college of my choice."

"She'll come round, when your grades don't drop and you don't turn into a dope fiend."

"Who has *time* to be a dope fiend?"

Jennifer began the rounds, thanking each Zodiac member personally for proposing her as a new member. Then she headed back to the library.

"Jennifer's really nice," Abby said to Cathy. "Penny and J.L. were impressed; she's funny when she wants to be. And nicer than they thought, too."

"I'm glad they're getting to know her," Cathy answered. "And I hope you like her, Abby. I feel funny, nominating a new member. In a way, you were the one who got the club started—maybe you should be the one to bring in the first new member."

"*I* have no objections to Jennifer being first."

"Meaning?"

Abby hesitated. "Jessica—I can't say she's thrilled about having Danny Burns's ex-girlfriend in the club."

"Not 'ex' for long, either," Cathy said. "I hope Jess

realizes there's a chance they could get back together again."

"Who knows what Jess thinks? She talks about Danny constantly, and she's convinced he's interested in her. You saw him dancing with her at J.L.'s party."

"That's nothing. Besides, he was obviously trying to make Jen jealous."

"Convince Jessica of that. All I'm saying is, it may take Jess awhile to accept Jennifer. Be prepared. And I can't blame her, either—everyone likes Danny."

There was a round of applause and Cathy and Abby turned in time to see J.L.'s mother accepting the Starscope money on behalf of the Oak Tree Center.

"It's pretty ironic that you thought of Starscope and you'll be the only one of us not in Danny's article," Abby said.

"What's more ironic is that Jennifer's trying to convince her parents what a worthwhile friend I am, and it'll look like I had nothing to do with this entire project. I'm glad we made money for the Center, but to tell the truth, I'm really relieved it's all over. Maybe things can go back to normal now."

"I hope."

It was an exhilarating ending for Starscope. Everyone was pleased—Harlan had received all the publicity and goodwill he needed to get Computer Capers off the ground; J.L.'s mother was thoroughly impressed with the job her daughter's club had done; and the staff at Oak Tree had signed a huge thank-you card for the Zodiacs.

"I can't thank you enough," Harlan said. "You've given Computer Capers more publicity than I dreamed of. The least I can do is treat you all to dinner."

"You could give Will a raise," Cathy suggested jokingly.

"I may have to," Harlan said. "In fact, I'd like to use your idea for a holiday promotion—you know, giving out horoscopes that suggest gifts for every sign? Maybe you girls would consider coming back."

"We'll discuss it," J.L. said hastily—thinking about all the things she had planned to do around the holidays.

"Don't panic, anyone," Will assured them. "I could probably handle that myself as a regular employee."

"Good," J.L. said. "I have plans for my free time for a while."

"How about we split for the diner," Will suggested.

It took just a few minutes to organize into cars and get to the diner. Danny made the most out of being one of two guys with six girls.

"I think we've had it with the sexist jokes," J.L. said. Her tone was unmistakably serious.

"*Excuse* me," Danny drawled. "I didn't mean to insult the liberated women present."

"You really don't like being sex objects?" Will asked teasingly.

"Cut it out," Cathy warned.

"You know," Danny said thoughtfully, "if you expect to be treated in a nonsexist way, you have to act that way too."

"What way?" J.L. sat back indignantly.

"Like treating men as equals," he said casually.

"Is someone treating you like a sex object?" J.L. asked— glancing directly at Jessica, who glared back at her.

"Not exactly," Danny said evasively. "But you haven't treated me like a real friend, either."

"What do you mean by that?" Cathy and Abby exchanged wary looks.

"I have a feeling this is going to be good," Will said.

"We *are* treating you like a real friend, Danny." Jessica raised her Coke glass hastily. "A toast—to our friend Danny Burns, who made Starscope such a success."

"Hey, thanks a lot," Penny complained. "We had something to do with it too."

"Of course," Jessica said shamefacedly. "I just meant a *special* thanks to Danny." She turned her big green eyes toward him. "Is that better?"

"Not exactly."

"We've been friendly. I don't get it," Jessica said.

"Especially Jess," J.L. joked. Penny jabbed her in the ribs.

"Actually, you've all discriminated against me," Danny said mournfully.

"What?" Cathy and Abby were suspicious; Penny and J.L. outraged; Jessica worried.

Elizabeth sat forward. "Why don't you explain," she said calmly.

"It's totally obvious. Not one of you asked me to be a Zodiac—yet."

"A what?" J.L. roared.

All talk stopped; all action ceased. And after a surprised silence, all heads turned to Danny.

He smiled charmingly. "Why not? I fit in. I work well with all of you, we have fun together . . . and I'm a Taurus and you don't have a Taurus member."

"Wait a minute. It's Jennifer," Cathy said. "She's a Taurus, as you know. We asked her to be a member."

"Well, can't there be two Tauruses? One girl, one boy?"

"But we don't have boys in the club," J.L. protested.

"You don't *yet*," Danny corrected her.

"That's outrageous," J.L. burst out.

"It's crazy," Cathy said firmly.

"Why?" Danny asked calmly. "Why is it crazy?"

"We're an all-girls club," Cathy sputtered. "It's for close friends—boys would ruin it, change it."

"How?" Danny appealed to Elizabeth. "You haven't said

anything. What do you think?"

"I think it makes sense," Jessica answered before Elizabeth could reply. "I think it's ungrateful not to ask you to join." She sat back beaming, thinking the subject closed.

"Elizabeth," Danny insisted.

Cathy turned to Elizabeth confidently. She knew how Elizabeth would feel.

Elizabeth's brow was furrowed. She pushed her long blond hair back from her face and cast Cathy a worried look. "I know you won't believe this, but it makes sense to me."

"Elizabeth!" Cathy gasped.

Abby sat back in shock. J.L. glared at her. Only Jessica seemed pleased.

"Danny has a point," Elizabeth said earnestly. "We aren't fair—we can't discriminate against him because he's a boy. He deserves it as much as Jennifer does."

"More," Jessica said.

Penny chimed in. "I think she's right. I hate to say it; I thought this was a girls' club too—but Danny deserves to be in *more* than Jennifer."

Cathy turned to Elizabeth. "I'm shocked. I can't believe this."

"Wait a minute."

Everyone turned to look at Abby. "Being fair isn't the point. Logic isn't the point. Danny did a great job with Starscope. We owe him a lot for that. But we're forgetting what the Zodiac Club is all about—it's about friends, who happen to be girls. No matter what you say, it would change if we let boys in."

"I agree totally," Cathy declared.

"I think I agree with both of you," Penny wailed. "This is confusing."

"Sure it's confusing," Danny said. "But listen to Elizabeth."

"Listen to Abby," Cathy declared. "It's not about who

deserves anything. I thought we wanted a club for girls."

"Even so," Elizabeth said, "there are plenty of clubs with both boys and girls and they're fun. Like the clubs at school."

"That's true," Penny said. "The camera club, the music and art clubs—they're all coed and it hasn't ruined them."

"Of course not." Jessica was thrilled to have Penny on her side. "It makes them more fun," she said fervently. "It's unnatural to be a one-sex group. The world is two sexes, after all."

"Don't you want to know what I think?" Will took off his glasses and polished them slowly.

"I'm not sure," Cathy admitted.

"I'm not sure either," Will told her. "On the one hand, I agree with Danny. Boys and girls should have clubs together, and sports—any activity. If we're going to treat each other as equals through life, we may as well start here. I like having girls as friends—lots of guys never learn to think of girls as people, and that's wrong."

"Then you agree with Danny," Jessica said happily.

"I agree in theory," Will continued, "but on the other hand, I like being with a group of guys too. It *is* different. When you're with your own sex you're more relaxed—maybe it's just that you have more in common."

"So which is it, Will?"

"I think it's up to you girls to decide. But if you want boys in the Zodiac Club, then I think I ought to be invited too."

"Oh, no," Cathy groaned. "I love having you around, Will. But we have to decide what we really want the most. We can always invite boys to meetings or Zodiac parties. So don't think we'll never have them around."

"That's a relief," J.L. joked.

"I just think our meetings should be all girls," Cathy finished.

"I agree," Abby said. "It's nice to be with all girls. No

one is self-conscious—you can really be yourself."

"That's gratitude for you," Danny said. "It didn't bother anyone that Will found the Starscope program for you and set up the Zodiac project with Harlan. Now, when it's time to relax, you don't want us around anymore."

"That's not what it is," Abby said. "We worked together on Starscope out of friendship. We couldn't have done it without Will or you—but these are two separate things."

"Look," Danny persisted, "isn't this fun? Right now, all of us sitting at the diner—why couldn't this be a club meeting? You girls can get together on your own at other times. Together, we can dream up more projects—maybe even take trips or do things you wouldn't have done."

"Will," Cathy appealed, reaching for one of his hands, "would you feel excluded personally if we said no boys allowed?"

"If something's important to you, I'd like to share it," Will said. "But we don't share everything, and maybe we each need our own time alone with friends. I can't say one way is better than the other."

Abby rescued Cathy. "Maybe we should stop before this gets too confusing. Mara's not here anyway, so we can't make official decisions or vote on the idea. Let's all think it over for a while. Maybe we need a meeting to hear both sides and vote on it." She swiveled in her seat. "How 'bout it, Danny? Is that fair?"

Danny mulled it over. "You are going to take me seriously—not pretend to forget about this?"

"We're serious." Jessica's eyes blazed. "You made a good point."

"Of course we'll be serious," Elizabeth echoed.

"Wait a minute." Cathy hesitated. "What about Jennifer? Is she still up for membership, or is it a choice between her and Danny now?"

"It's not a choice," Abby said firmly. The other girls agreed—except for Jessica, who agreed reluctantly. "How many new members can we take?" she grumbled.

Cathy eyed her closely. "We'll decide that at our next meeting. I don't think this should be a contest." She couldn't help glancing at Danny when she said it, but he seemed unfazed by her comment.

"We all agree, then," Abby said. "We'll meet next week to decide who we'll consider for membership."

Cathy and Will walked together toward Will's car.

"You're not mad, are you, Cathy?"

"I don't know."

"Danny's point is logical."

"Logical to you, Will," she said coolly, "but to Danny it's more than that. That's why I'm upset. Wait here." Cathy turned, searching for Danny's tall figure on the street. Seeing him bending to unlock his car door, she hurried to his side before Will had a chance to reply.

"Danny, wait."

Danny straightened up and smiled. "Cathy, I'm glad you stopped to talk. You seemed upset in there. Believe me, it's nothing personal against you. I'm not a troublemaker— I think I'm right. Don't forget, you girls are great people— I enjoy being with all of you."

"I want to be sure of something. Are you doing this to hurt Jennifer?"

"What?"

"I shouldn't butt in, but I care about her and, well, if you'd stopped to notice maybe you'd see that she—"

"You should talk about hurting people," Danny interrupted curtly. "What about your hurting Will?"

"What?"

"The both of you, you and Jennifer. When I think of you . . ." Danny's eyes reflected the hurt he had felt overhearing the girls' conversation about their escapades—whiskey and sneaking around. "How could you do that to Will and then act so cozy with him?"

Cathy was totally bewildered. "I have no idea what you're talking about. Does Will look like I've hurt him?"

Will was waiting patiently for Cathy by his car. When he saw them both glance his way, he smiled and waved.

"Poor guy," Danny said. "No—he's not hurt yet. He hasn't heard about your escapades, but I have."

"Danny, I'm missing something here, but maybe you should know..." She paused helplessly. What should she say? It wasn't her place to say that Jennifer still liked him—even if Cathy knew it was true. Somehow, she had to warn Danny not to blow it this time. "Maybe you should drop the Zodiac Club membership push, so Jen won't think..."

"Won't think what?"

Cathy struggled to find the right words. She gave one last try. "You know the old saying—'You can catch more flies with honey...'"

"You've lost me, Cathy. You want me to sweet-talk the Zodiacs about this?"

"Not the Zodiacs, someone else, someone who wants to be caught..."

"If you mean Jessica," Danny started to protest, "she's a nice kid, but—"

"Not Jessica! This is hopeless!"

"Look, there's another old saying. 'Do unto others'—maybe you and your partner should keep that in mind on your next midnight outing."

Will had gotten in his car and now he pulled up alongside Danny's car. "Cathy, are you coming or what?"

Cathy shot Danny one last helpless look before getting into Will's car. "I'll explain another time," she said lamely.

"Sure...fine." Danny helped to shut her door, leaning

in to say good night again to Will. "Will, boy, maybe you can pick up Cathy's vote," he joked. "I think I've lost it."

Cathy smiled weakly as they pulled away.

"What was that all about?"

Cathy sighed. "About me and my big mouth. I was trying to play matchmaker, but I really screwed up."

"Matchmaker?"

"I guess I can tell you. I was trying to smooth the way for Danny and Jen to get back together."

"So that's it! I thought you were trying to get him to drop his Zodiac idea."

"No, it's not that. After all, I'm only one out of seven. My opinion won't change things. No, I'm upset because of Jennifer."

"She'll be angry Danny wants to be in the club *she* wants to join."

"She'll be hurt," Cathy corrected. "Jen doesn't want things to go on like this with Danny. Wait till she hears he wants to be in the club! She might even drop out if he joins."

"I don't see how you can help. Sounds like they've already blown their chance of getting back together."

"I have a plan that could work," Cathy said. "If only I knew whether Danny was interested. Do you think he is?"

"He's never said anything about her to me," Will said.

"I need more than that. Do you think he likes her— even a little?"

Will nodded reluctantly. "I think so. But he'd never tell me so. And he won't drop this membership thing. Would that hurt your plan?"

"That doesn't matter. If we're right, if Danny and Jen still care about each other, being in the club or not won't mean a thing."

"So tell me your plan."

"I'll have to check it with Jen first."

Will leaned back from the wheel to get a better look at Cathy. "I haven't seen you this revved up in weeks. This is the old Cathy!"

"I know." But Cathy furrowed her brow. "There's something peculiar, though."

"What?"

"Did you tell Danny about the other night when we made up?"

"You mean your ridiculous kidnapping escapade? No, I didn't tell him. It's kind of personal, don't you think?"

"That's it! 'Escapade'—that word rang a bell." Cathy turned to him excitedly. "You didn't tell Danny anything about it, but he knows something."

"I just said that we'd made up. So?"

"Danny must have overheard something about the escapade."

"Where?"

"Probably from me and Jen." Cathy's eyes grew wide and she laughed out loud. "Oh no! Now I understand everything—'drinking and running around'—this is too much!"

"Cathy, you're incoherent." Will pulled the car over to the curb.

"I'm not hysterical. It's just so funny."

Will looked mildly annoyed. "Mind letting me in on the joke?"

When Cathy's laughing fit subsided, she explained, "Danny overheard Jen and me talking at the paper. In fact, I know the exact day it happened, too. Remember the water pistol loaded with whiskey?"

Will nodded. "How could I forget?"

"Jen and I were joking about getting caught that night—with liquor—after we'd been out kidnapping boys and kissing at midnight! Jen was talking about you and me, but Danny must have thought she and I were sneaking around, drinking and making out with other boys. Danny practically accused me of two-timing you tonight. He thinks I'm terrible!" She fell into a fit of helpless laughter again. But this time, Will laughed too.

"That explains everything. Danny dropped a few hints that you weren't entirely honest—I couldn't figure it out either. Now I get it."

"Oh, Will, it's funny, but it's so awful! You've got to explain everything to him."

"It's sort of embarrassing," Will said.

"We all acted dumb," Cathy said. "But this could be a blessing in disguise. If you talk to Danny and I talk to Jennifer, we'll straighten it all out."

"I tell you what. Call Jennifer from that pay phone and see if she's home. I'll drive over now—it's still early. I can drop you at Jen's while I go to Danny's."

Cathy hurried to the pay phone on the corner and made the call. Jennifer hesitated when Cathy asked to come by, but said okay.

"It's okay," Cathy reported to Will. "Drive me to Jen's."

"I'll pick you up in half an hour."

"Great," Cathy said. "It's best if I explain everything to her now. No wonder Danny's been so cool to us both lately— it's so funny. I'll tell her about him wanting to join Zodiac, too. Our big misunderstanding is over. I'll bet my plan will work after all."

"Sounds good to me. I'll square things with Danny as best I can."

Cathy squeezed Will's hand. "Keep your fingers crossed."

15 ★

Danny peered through the small windows of the front door.

"Will—what's up?"

"I'd like to talk. I've got some explaining to do, on Cathy's behalf."

"Sure. I'm on the phone right now, but come on in. Everyone's out so we've got the place to ourselves."

Danny led Will into the brightly lit kitchen, where the phone receiver lay on the table. Danny put his hand over the receiver, motioning for Will to sit down.

"Mara? Sorry for the interruption. As I was saying, I'm sure you'll hear about it from J.L., but I wanted to personally tell you my reasons for joining the club."

Danny listened to Mara while Will got up and rattled through the refrigerator for a cold soda.

"That's right. I thought you'd get my point. You seem pretty openminded...right....Listen, I'll be glad to talk more about it. And maybe you'd like to ask Will any questions—he'll see you in school tomorrow, won't he?"

Will signaled "No," but Danny was already saying goodbye.

"Campaigning already?"

"I wanted Mara to hear it from me first." Danny grinned, rubbing his hands together. "The first call of many—I'm launching an all-out campaign. I have to do most of it by phone, but you—you lucky man—you're in school with these girls every day! What an opportunity. I'd have posters, if I were you: 'Zodiacs Unfair to Males' and 'Female Chauvinists on the Loose.' Really hit 'em hard on the sexism thing—call it reverse discrimination. They'll be afraid not to let you in the club."

"Danny, I don't want to do that."

"Too nasty? Too aggressive?" Danny scowled. "Okay, we'll think of something milder, more suited to your temperament."

"Hold it—style isn't the problem."

"Well, are we in this thing together or not?" Danny took another gulp. "We want a free society, don't we?" His eyes twinkled.

"I only want to be in the Zodiacs if Cathy wants me there. If they all vote for a boy-girl club, sure, I'll join. But so what if they want an all-girls thing? I don't care."

"You're not campaigning, then?"

"Not me. I'll support you, and if they vote to let guys in, I'll probably join—though I've got plenty to do without their club.

"Takes some of the fun away if you're not into it," Danny said. "But, okay, I see your point."

"Anyway, that's not why I'm here."

"Something about Cathy?"

"There's been a small misunderstanding." Will cleared his throat, caught between a blush and a nervous laugh. Danny looked at him curiously.

"You said something about an escapade to Cathy today. She's embarrassed that you got the wrong idea about her. See, when we made up... well, *that* was the escapade. It was Cathy and me. Cathy 'kidnapped' me while Jennifer stood guard." Will went on to describe the whole scene, including the whiskey-filled water pistol. When he finished, Danny gaped at him without saying a word.

"That was their wicked adventure?"

"Well, it *was* for them," Will said. "They could have gotten in big trouble—especially Jennifer."

"Yeah, it was brave of her, considering her parents."

"You bet. I guess you know how great Jen is. Cathy will be glad we cleared this up. She couldn't bear you thinking of her as a cheat or a sneak. She and Jen haven't gone out with other boys. I don't know why Jennifer isn't going with anyone."

Danny stared vacantly at Will. "Yeah, going with anyone. Well. So you're the mystery boy...there's no secret drinking...running wild, lying..."

Will glanced slyly at Danny. "Those girls are really terrific. Don't you agree?"

Jennifer answered the door on the first ring. She motioned for Cathy to go up to her room without stopping first to say hello to her parents.

Cathy waited for Jennifer to close the door before speaking. "What's the matter? Your folks not speaking tonight?"

"I'm not supposed to have any visitors. You can only stay fifteen minutes."

"Oh, no—I don't like the sound of this."

"Well, last night...I confessed."

"To what?"

"To midnight madness," Jennifer said wryly. "I told them the truth about being out the other night."

Cathy stopped in the middle of unbuttoning her jacket to stare at Jennifer in horror.

"You didn't!"

"I did."

Cathy was stunned. "But...then, why did they let me come over? Aren't they furious? This isn't a trap, is it?"

Jennifer almost laughed. "No trap. They were more shocked at my lying to them than anything else. Mom especially—she felt really bad that I was so afraid to talk to her. I mean, they're furious—'really disappointed' is how she put it. I'm grounded for the week."

"You're kidding."

"I told them they made me feel I had to lie, that they didn't realize I needed friends and that friendship involves responsibility. After all, you're my friend and you were unhappy and I wanted to help you. It's not like I did something terrible."

"They must have loved that."

"They said there was nothing wrong with my wanting to help you, but I shouldn't have lied. I don't know—I felt sick about sneaking, and the lies kept getting more complicated. I'm relieved I told."

"This is awful."

"They said they want what's best for me," Jennifer said. "I said they didn't know the kind of pressure I felt."

"Maybe the Starscope article will help," Cathy said. "Would they like the Zodiac Club any better if they read good things about it?"

"They might be impressed, though of course the first thing they'll say is, 'Why didn't *I* write it?'"

"You wrote an article too," Cathy pointed out.

Jennifer shrugged. "They're just like that. Anyway, they're not too pleased with me right now."

"I feel awful being here. I lied to them too."

"I told them it was all my idea, and it was," Jennifer insisted. "You're in the clear."

"Still, I wish I could prove I'm not a sneak."

"It's okay—believe me."

"I hope you're allowed to go out by next weekend," Cathy said. "This could ruin everything."

"What's next weekend?"

Cathy took a deep breath. "There's good news and bad news. Which do you want first?"

"The bad," Jennifer said suspiciously. "What is it?"

"Don't get upset, but Danny thought it might be a good

idea if the Zodiacs proved how modern and openminded they are by, uh, letting a discriminated group into the club."

"Who've you discriminated against?"

"Well . . . boys."

"Boys?"

"To be specific"—Cathy swallowed—"Danny wants to be a Zodiac."

Jennifer's face was totally expressionless. "A Zodiac."

"Well, he has a point—after all, there are plenty of coed clubs around, and he does get along with everyone . . ."

Jennifer's mouth pursed. "Why does he have to do everything I do? Can't he just leave me alone; won't it ever end?"

"Jen, wait—let me tell you the rest. The good news, remember?"

"I can't believe he'd do this to me."

"Jen, he's not all bad, is he?"

"Why are you sticking up for him?"

"I'm beginning to really like the guy. Listen to this— it's really kind of sweet," Cathy began. A giggle escaped. "He thought . . ." Another giggle interrupted.

"What?"

"Our 'escapade'—he overheard us and he thought . . ." Cathy was laughing again, and one look at Jennifer's bewildered expression and she couldn't stop herself.

Jennifer stared at her as if she was crazy.

"Wait . . . I'll stop," Cathy gasped. She swallowed hard and held her breath. "All right."

"What is going on?"

One last peal of laughter rang out and then Cathy got hold of herself. "You'll laugh too, Jen. Remember that day at the paper, when you and I were talking about kissing boys in the moonlight, and getting rid of the booze, and sneaking out late at night? Remember?"

"This is the good news?"

"Wait. Remember how you said Danny was acting even stranger after that day—and he was even cold to me . . . remember you noticed that?"

"So?"

"You're going to love this." Cathy took a deep breath. "Do you remember at the paper, we were talking about our 'midnight escapade'?"

Jennifer nodded.

"Danny was listening to us the whole time. He didn't know we were talking about Will and me, and he thought you and I were sneaking out at night to be with wild boys."

A corner of Jen's mouth lifted slightly. "And dumping whiskey down the drain afterward?"

"You should have heard him telling me off—he put me down for cheating on Will, being a sneak . . ." Cathy started laughing again and Jennifer chuckled along with her.

"He thought you did that? And you . . ." They were both laughing now. Cathy wiped her eyes and said soberly, "Seriously—you get what this means."

"What?"

"Danny was very upset about you doing that, Jen. I think that's the sign you needed, that he still likes you."

"Maybe."

"No maybes about it. He cares. And I think I can get you two back together."

"How? Especially now. I can't see him except in school."

"I owe you a plan, right?"

"Right."

"I have one. But it means you have to really swallow your pride."

"I don't know."

"You have to decide."

"I don't know. Now it looks like Danny will get to be in the Zodiacs and I won't. It's so typical of him—I'm so fed up. How do I forgive him?"

"I think you want to."

"But he's doing it to me again—competing for the sak
of winning. Why should I swallow my pride?"

"Remember what you told me once—how both of yo
wanted to work together at the *Chronicle?* How do you know
Danny doesn't want that with the Zodiacs? He still think
you're joining, and you may be. Maybe he wants to be clos
to you—not to compete, to share."

"Then you must want boys in the club."

"I don't, but it won't kill me if it happens. But you'r
changing the subject."

"I know."

"Don't worry about Danny and the Zodiac Club. Thi
will all blow over, and you two should be together."

"Meaning what?"

"Meaning you either take Danny as he is or not at all."
Jennifer checked her watch. "You've got to go now."

"Will is picking me up in fifteen minutes—he's at Dan
ny's now. I guess I'll sit outside and wait."

"What's he doing at Danny's?"

"Trying to clear my name."

"And mine?"

"And talking about Zodiacs, probably." Cathy sighed
"How did everything get so complicated? You do something
for one person and you end up hurting somebody else."

"I don't know." Jennifer held the bedroom door open
From downstairs they could hear the sound of her mother's
typewriter; her father was talking on the phone. "It is complicated. But I'm glad you came by. Tell the other girls
why I can't see them this week. I guess that ends the Zodiacs
for me. Danny will get in for sure and I'll be left out."

Cathy grasped her arm reassuringly. "Look, I guess I
won't see you till Monday."

"Guess not. But at least I've got the *Chronicle* to look
forward to. See you then."

Cathy went outside to wait for Will. It felt like forever before Will came and she got in the warm car gratefully.

"Everything's going great," he announced. "I cleared Jen's name—you should have seen Danny's face when I told him it was you and me kissing at midnight. What relief!"

"It doesn't matter, Will. Jen got caught—I mean she confessed. She told her parents the truth and now she's grounded. No calls, no friends—she's not going to join Zodiacs. She's not real crazy about Danny getting in the club when she can't."

"What about your big plan?"

"What's the use? She's not interested in Danny now. Forget it."

"Cath, don't take it so hard."

"Why not?" Cathy said crossly. "I'm so mad at myself."

"It's not your fault."

"I feel like it is."

"Why?"

"If it wasn't for me, Jen wouldn't have been sneaking around—that's why. I kicked her out of Zodiacs before she even got in. How did this mess start, anyhow?"

"Cathy, forget it. Look, whatever happens now, happens. It's out of your hands, so let it go."

"Leos don't let things go."

They both watched the road until Cathy spoke again.

"Jen told her parents that friendship is responsibility. She's right. She put herself out for me and got in big trouble. I can't let it go. It's my responsibility."

"Fine. What are you going to do?"

Cathy threw her hands up hopelessly. "I have no idea."

They had reached Cathy's house.

"Want me to come in for a minute? Watch TV or something?"

"I'm not great company, Will. I'll see you tomorrow."

Cathy leaned over for a good-night kiss.

"Thanks, Will. Sorry to be such a pain—I'll make it up to you. We'll do something fun tomorrow, just the two of us."

Will shook his head fondly. "Being with you is never boring. I'll see you tomorrow—and cheer up."

Jane was sitting up watching a comedy show. Her parents were half-watching and half-reading. Cathy said hello and good night in one breath and climbed wearily to her room.

"Okay," she said to herself sternly, "enough feeling sorry for yourself. Think, girl—what's the plan now?"

But no bright ideas clicked into place. Finally she decided to sleep on it. She had to think of some way to fix things. There wasn't much time.

The phone rang. Her father picked it up downstairs.

"Cathy—for you. Keep it short, it's late."

"Who is it?"

The voice boomed cheerfully in her ear. "Danny here. Sorry it's late—your folks said you were out earlier but they let me call back 'cause it's important."

"Danny?"

"Got a minute? Thought we'd talk about the Zodiac Club."

His voice was bright and eager.

"Danny, it's late. Not now."

Cathy started to hang up, but his voice piped louder through the receiver, as if he guessed her thoughts.

"Wait—I know I get carried away sometimes, but I really called about something else."

Cathy waited.

"Jennifer can't get calls right now," he said. "So I was wondering . . ."

Cathy briefly explained why Jennifer was being punished.

"Oh." Danny hesitated. "It was real nice, what Jen did for you and Will. I'm sorry she's in trouble."

"We all are."

"Well, maybe you could tell her I said so—when you see her."

"Danny, you'll see her before I do. I won't see her till work Monday and you'll be at school with her."

"We don't talk much at school nowadays."

"Maybe you should start."

There was a moment of silence on Danny's end. "I've gotta go, it's late."

"I know, Danny."

"Okay. We can talk about your vote some other time."

Cathy chuckled as she hung up. Despite the way he annoyed her, Danny's good intentions had a way of shining through, making her forgive him. She had to admit she was growing fonder of him—but she still didn't want him, or any boy, in her club.

_____ 16 ★

The unhatched plan troubled Cathy. It was Monday. All afternoon she watched Danny and Jennifer at the *Chronicle*. Maybe Danny seemed slightly less distant toward Jen, and just maybe—unless it was Cathy's imagination—Jen was less resentful in her manner toward Danny. But as far as getting them back together, it still seemed hopeless.

Cathy could hardly blame them. She had helped ruin their chances of making up. She stared glumly at the stack of papers in front of her. It was almost time to go home and she had barely made it through them. She was searching for fillers—small pieces, funny or light, to fill the extra spaces between columns.

The phone on her desk rang and she jumped, startled out of her reverie. The caller asked for Danny Burns.

"He's not at this phone," Cathy explained. "If you'll wait I'll go find him—he's here somewhere."

"He must be there," the caller said crankily. "He left this number to call."

The voice sounded familiar to Cathy. "Mara, is that you?"

"Who's this—Cathy?"

"I didn't expect you on the line."

"Me either. But I'd rather talk to you than Burns."

"What's up?"

"It's Danny and his crazy phone calls! He's driving everyone nuts with this phone campaign—even at school."

"School?"

"J.L. was walking down the hall today and a pay phone rang. It was Danny Burns saying, 'Don't discriminate against men—vote Burns for Zodiacs.'"

"He is crazy."

"How'd you like to get calls from him before you get up in the morning?"

"Or last thing at night? Tell me about it."

"He must want to be in the club a lot."

"Have you decided how to vote yet?"

"No, I'm waiting for Saturday's meeting."

"He should be in politics," Cathy cracked.

"I pity the country that lets Burns run for office. Think of the telephone bills!"

Cathy laughed. "Should I give him that message?"

"Yeah—and tell him my father says give him a break."

"Got it."

"See ya, Cathy."

Cathy smiled as she hung up the phone. It felt good to laugh at Mara's story, but she couldn't tell Jennifer. Any mention of Danny's campaign either sent Jennifer off on an angry tirade or made her sulky. Cathy sighed. How had all this started?

She thought about all that happened and how competition and pressure were the cause. Rivalry had kept Jen and Danny apart and created trouble for everyone. There was no way to say who started it or who was to blame.

"That's quite a scowl," Helen, the receptionist, said as she passed Cathy's desk. "Finishing a story before deadline?"

"No, no..." Cathy gazed at the woman thoughtfully. "Helen, you raised five daughters. Was rivalry ever a problem for them? I mean seriously—did they get caught up in competition?"

"Did they ever," Helen said. "It's no joking matter—there's plenty of it among sisters, and some of it never ends. Believe me, I know how much damage it can cause."

"And not only that," Cathy said more to herself than Helen, "think of the other pressures on kids: parents telling them to get good grades, to get into the best college, pressure from their friends to go along with the crowd..."

"I used to tell my kids that competition wasn't so important. I liked them to do their best, but not go crazy trying to be better than each other; they had enough to worry about. And I think they did all right. They each have what they wanted—a good job, or a family or both, like my youngest two. But everyone is different—some are willing to pay the price for what they want. You're not having a hard time, are you, Cathy? This job too much pressure for you?"

Cathy quickly assured her she was all right. "But, Helen, sometimes I think the pressure we put on ourselves is the worst kind."

Helen patted Cathy's shoulder kindly and walked on down the hall.

Cathy began writing: *Pressure harms everyone. It makes people feel isolated. Pressures sometimes mount so high that kids contemplate actually ending their misery.*

It's hard enough to grow up, Cathy continued, *with all the expectations on a person. Kids have to deal with so much at once. They get a mixed message from adults who believe competition is healthy but don't want kids to be cutthroat.*

Competition cheats people because it takes up the good time and chokes off that space needed for healthy growth. Kids should think more of achieving excellence for its own sake. Parents should give kids enough time and space to breathe and develop themselves.

Friendship is part of that development and it includes responsibility. Making and keeping friends is a personal choice based on important needs and sometimes means as much as family ties. Friends are an important part of kids' lives and adults should try to comprehend this.

Cathy poured her feelings out.

"Aren't you leaving, Cathy?" Helen interrupted her. "It's late."

Startled, Cathy looked around. She hadn't even seen anyone take off.

"Is it that late?" Cathy glanced down at the paper. "I got carried away, I guess. I wrote a piece on competition."

"Is it for Mrs. Mead to read?"

"It's nothing. I mean, it's not polished, it's just what I was thinking."

"May I take a look?" Helen reached toward the page.

"It's not really ready, but I guess if you want, you can." Cathy picked up the few fillers she thought might be most useful and walked them down the hall to the night editor's desk. When she got back to the newsroom, Helen was sitting with her coat on, immersed in the essay.

"It's just notes." Cathy reached for her jacket and pocketbook and got ready to leave.

"What are you doing with this piece?" Helen asked.

"Nothing—I hadn't thought about it. It was just something I had to get out of my system."

"It's quite well done. I think I know someone who might find it interesting. May I show it to someone else?"

"Sure, go ahead. But it's not written that well..."

"It's straight from the heart," Helen declared. "You should be proud of it. Here..." Helen held the sheet out. "Put your name on this."

"I don't have to really." Cathy smiled doubtfully.

"Do you believe in what you said?"

"Absolutely."

"Well?"

Cathy wrote her name at the top of the page. "If you show it to your daughters," she said, heading for the door, "they might not appreciate my advice, but I think it will give them something to think about!"

"Hattie?" Helen knocked as she poked her head in Mrs. Mead's office. "Can I show you something?"

Mara came running toward the group gathered under the maple trees. It was another crisp, cool morning.

"Here's the Starscope story!" Mara cried.

"The *Chronicle,* already?"

"Ours is delivered early." Mara gasped, nearly out of breath. "Wait till you see it; it's gorgeous."

"Hurry, before the bell rings."

Mara spilled her books onto the ground, ignoring them. "Here—it's in the back in that separate section." They crushed around her, peering over her shoulders.

"Sorry you're not in the pictures," Mara said to Cathy.

"That's okay. It looks great!"

Danny's story had gotten a full spread, including photos.

J.L. moaned. "Look at me—I look awful. Why didn't you tell me I needed a haircut?"

Jessica's eyes sparkled. "I love fame! I love it! Cathy, get us extra copies."

"Let me see." Penny took the paper from Jessica's hands. "Your lover boy Danny did a super job—the Zodiacs sound impressive: 'group of dedicated young women . . . devoting time and effort . . . generous . . . pretty.'" Penny looked up giggling. "He pours it on, doesn't he?"

"Give it back. And he's not my lover boy," Jessica said emphatically.

"It's over already? What happened?" Mara asked.

"Oh, nothing. He's more interested in friendship."

"Jess asked him over for a private briefing," J.L. teased. "Scared him off, huh?"

"Shows you how ungrateful boys are," Jessica sniffed. "Virgos need real appreciation."

"You mean, they like boys they can push around."

"J.L.," Abby said, "Jess meant well."

"He lost my vote." Jessica put a hand on Cathy's arm. "If Jennifer still wants him, she's welcome to him."

"Are you sure?" J.L. held out the Starscope pictures again. "You're famous now, your name in print—aren't you being ungrateful?"

Jessica turned away haughtily. "I've got other fish to fry."

"But you like boys, Jess—not fish." J.L. followed her into the school, teasing mercilessly.

"What are you looking for, Cathy?" Abby watched as Cathy leafed through the rest of the paper.

"Jen and I did an article that should be in this week. On renovating ware . . ."

She stopped in mid-sentence, gaping at the page in front of her.

"What're you looking at?"

Abby leaned over, pushing the paper down so she could read over Cathy's shoulder.

"Cathy, your hands are trembling," Penny said. "What is it?"

"'IS WINNING WORTH THE PRICE?'" Abby read out loud. "'By Cathy Rosen, *Chronicle* intern.'"

Cathy turned stunned eyes to her friends. "The editorial page," she gasped.

"Let me see!" Penny grabbed the paper away. "It's a guest editorial—I'm impressed."

"Cathy, you never told us." Abby shook Cathy's arm. "Hey, wake up...are you there?"

"I'm shocked. I never...Oh..." She suddenly knew who Helen's friend was and realized how the piece had gotten published—Mrs. Mead.

"Cathy, this is terrific," Penny exclaimed, holding the paper for them all to see. "I hope every teacher in school reads this."

"Read it to me," Abby demanded.

Penny began, "'Everyone loses, and everyone suffers from the pressures of competition...'"

"Is it all yours?" Mara gazed at Cathy in admiration.

"Every word—except for the title." Cathy's shock was wearing off—pride setting in instead. "Let me see it again, Penny."

Cathy read it over to herself. "It seems so official in the paper. And polished."

"It has authority," Abby said.

"Can I keep this copy?" Cathy asked Mara.

"If you let me read it before homeroom," Mara teased.

Cathy floated happily through the day. Will met her as usual at lunchtime. "It's wonderful, Cath. Everyone's heard about it—we all want autographed copies!"

"Thanks." Cathy beamed at him. Being a celebrity was thrilling—her English teacher had read the piece aloud to her class, and then the principal had called Cathy into her office to congratulate her personally and gave her a note for her parents.

"I'm going to call Helen the receptionist and thank her," Cathy told Will. "She did it. And I'll thank Mrs. Mead too. What a day! I wonder if Jennifer's seen it yet?" Cathy frowned. "What if she thinks I sneaked the piece in behind her back? Danny and I have our own stories in and Jen only has the story she wrote with me."

"Hey, dummy." Will put his hands on her shoulders, stopping her in her tracks. "Listen to your own advice—stop keeping score. Jennifer will be happy for you. She's had her moments, and she will again. Enjoy it—be proud of yourself."

"Thanks, Will. It's hard to remember my own advice!"

When she got home, her parents added their congratulations—beaming when Cathy read them the note from Mrs. Hopewell.

"Very nice," her mother said, "but why are you sitting here wasting time? Go study—raise your grades..."

"Oh, Ma." Cathy collapsed laughing. "You were never like that."

"A good thing, too. I'd be ashamed if I had, after reading this."

Jane burst in the back door, arms filled with copies of the *Chronicle*. "Dad's got ten more," she cried, dumping the pile of papers on the kitchen table. "Whew! We cleaned them out. It was so embarrassing—Dad admitted who you were—I could've died."

"Jane, we are all proud of your sister—they understand."

"It was gross," Jane insisted, "though your piece was real good, Cathy."

"Thanks." Cathy smiled. "Do you think we have enough copies for all our relatives now?"

Cathy's mother gave her a big hug. "Don't tease—we're proud."

The doorbell rang.

"Get that, Cath—if celebrities answer doors."

"Very funny."

Jennifer began chattering the moment the door opened. "Did you write that piece for me?"

"Jennifer! You're out of your house."

"Thanks to you." Jennifer enveloped Cathy in an enormous hug. "It's the best thing I've ever read."

"The best by an author who's friends with you."

"Stop kidding, it's true. My parents let me out of the house, didn't they?"

"My piece did that?"

"Between Danny's Starscope story raving about the wonderful civic-minded Zodiacs and your essay, they had no choice. Cathy, it's a wonderful piece. It's exactly how I felt—you said it for all of us. My parents said you're sensitive and insightful."

"Does this mean you can join the Zodiacs?"

"Do you still want me?"

"Jen"—Cathy grabbed her hands—"that's half the reason I wrote this thing."

Jennifer held out a package. "Look, it's a picture frame. My parents sent me over here so you could sign your piece. We're going to frame it and hang it where we can always see it!"

"Oh, Jennifer."

"When did you write it?"

"Monday, at work. I sat there and it spilled out. Helen asked me why I was staying so late. I showed it to her and she showed it to Mrs. Mead."

"People really like you, Cathy—that's important. Know who said that?"

"Who?"

"My parents."

"You're kidding."

"Nope. I'm telling you, they were impressed—you moved them."

Cathy looked at the picture frame in Jennifer's hands. "Come on in. If you really want, I'll sign this for you."

"By the way, that's not the only reason I came over."

"What else?"

"You had a plan . . ."

"You mean it? You're interested?"

"After reading this—you're right. The rivalry should stop somewhere, and somebody has to make the first move. I'm doing it in your honor."

"And getting Danny back has nothing to do with it?"

Jennifer actually blushed. "Maybe a little."

"This is great," Cathy shouted. "I love a challenge. Remember you and Danny have to swallow some pride."

"Okay, okay—I'm listening."

"What's the one thing Danny knows he can beat you at?"

Jennifer looked puzzled.

"What does Danny do that you don't do?"

"There's nothing. What—"

"Tennis," Cathy said emphatically.

"Tennis," Jennifer repeated.

"That's right."

"I don't get it."

"How's your tennis game?"

"Lousy, you know that."

"Right. You are going to challenge Danny Burns to a tennis match."

"You've gone off the deep end." Jennifer regarded Cathy with pity.

"Don't you see, Jen?"

"No. I can't play tennis with him—I'll lose."

"You want to lose. The match doesn't count—it's the message."

"What message? That I'm a jerk? Danny will laugh."

"Danny? Think about it—he'll eat it up. He'll either want to beat you to get even with you..."

"Or?"

"Or he'll see the challenge for what it is."

"Which is?"

"An admission. You're saying to Danny that you're willing to let him beat you. You know you can't win at tennis."

Jennifer thought it over. "You mean, Danny knows he'll win—he'll see it as an apology from me, a chance to even the score between us."

"Right."

"But what if he doesn't see that? What if he just beats me and gloats about it?"

"Then he's not worth caring for anymore."

"I'm not crazy about making a fool of myself."

"Jen..." Cathy sat next to her on the bed. "He plays tennis better than you. Does that make you a fool?"

"I'll have to think about it, okay?"

"I guess. I thought you'd love it—it's the best plan I came up with."

"I'll think about it. Promise."

In her room that night, Jennifer put down her physics notes and began rummaging through her closet, digging out old sneakers and a couple of flat tennis balls. Her racket was stuck in a back corner, wedged between her typewriter case and a dusty stack of notebooks. She wrestled it out and poked at the strings. It felt strange in her hands, but she shifted her weight to the balls of her feet, leaning forward from the hips. She took a few practice swipes, bringing the racket back slowly and carefully, trying not to drop the head—her worst habit.

More confidently, she leaned forward again, changing grips from forehand to backhand, stroking with ease. Suddenly it was simple—the racket was an extension of her arm, just like her teachers always said it should be. A sly grin spread across her face. If she was going to lose, she would look good doing it—and go down fighting.

—————————————————— **17 ★**

Cathy was ready for the big meeting. Everyone sat around Abby's living room.

Cathy took a deep breath and gave Jennifer a reassuring wink. Jennifer, Danny, and Will had all come to hear the decision. Instinctively, they had sat by themselves, out of the way—like prisoners waiting to hear their sentences.

"I don't exactly know the procedure," Abby said, unofficially taking over the meeting. "Maybe you three should wait outside."

Will stood up right away. "Actually, I'm out of it. I think you should keep Zodiacs the way it is—just for girls."

He left the room.

That left Jennifer and Danny, who did their best to avoid each other's eyes. Cathy was disappointed—she had expected Jen to call her, saying to put the plan into action. But when no call came, Cathy felt maybe it was time to give up.

J.L. raised her hand. "Maybe the candidates should speak—tell us why they want to be Zodiacs." She nodded at Jennifer, who looked like she'd rather be anywhere else.

"I hate talking about myself."

A spatter of encouraging laughter rang around the room.

Jennifer dropped her eyes. "I guess you all know—Cathy's piece was about someone very like me." She took a deep breath, and Cathy could see it took an effort for her to go on. "Maybe I haven't been around that much; I've probably been studying while you've all been together doing things. Meeting Cathy, and all of you, I've realized that I like people a lot. I like being around you guys. I guess I want to be a Zodiac so we can all be good friends. That's all."

Penny and Mara both started to applaud, but Abby stopped them.

"Danny?" she said. "Do you have anything to say?"

Danny started to get up, but J.L. blurted out, "Are you kidding? Do we have to listen to him again?"

Everyone burst out laughing. It was true—they'd all heard more than enough from Danny already.

"All those phone calls," Mara groaned. "I move Danny's not allowed to say another word."

"You two should wait outside now," Abby said. They got up and trooped out.

Finally Elizabeth broke the silence. "Let's do the easy part first. Let's vote on Jennifer."

Jessica squirmed uneasily. "I don't feel I know her well enough to vote."

"Jess," Elizabeth said firmly, "did you make an effort? Did you try to get to know her?"

"I could try again," Jessica said in a small voice. Cathy felt an urge to hug her.

"I don't know about all of you," Abby declared, "but I say yes—she's in."

"How could we say no?" Penny asked, and Mara and Elizabeth nodded in total agreement.

"Wait." Cathy stood up. "Don't say yes for the wrong reasons. Don't feel obliged. She's got a lot to offer."

"It's hard," Penny said carefully. "I feel like she needs us. But I like her—especially for the way she stood up for Cathy."

"That awful meeting," J.L. groaned, remembering. "Horrible."

"I accept Penny's reasons." Cathy grinned. "I'd forgotten that meeting. It *was* awful, and Jen was terrific."

"Spunky, I'd say," J.L. added.

"Class," Penny put in.

"All right, let's vote, then. All for Jennifer as our new Taurus?"

A show of hands, and Jennifer made it in—unanimously.

"You've got class too," Cathy whispered to Jessica. Jess smiled gratefully.

"Second vote," Abby announced. "Danny Burns's membership. Now, does accepting Danny mean we have to accept all boys—or just him?"

"All boys? What a thought! Danny is enough."

"If Will isn't interested, Danny would be the only boy," Abby said.

"I'm not going to go looking for other boys to join," J.L. drawled.

"Me either. Danny's okay, he's nice, but not just any boy would fit in." Mara was firm about it, her mouth grim and her arms crossed tight.

Elizabeth spoke. "If we can't think of other boys to join, it would be stupid to have Danny at all."

"Maybe he should be mascot," Jessica suggested.

"Maybe he should be our friend," Cathy said, "like Will."

"Cathy's right. We don't need to change the Zodiacs because we like Danny."

"He could come to our parties," Mara piped up.

"He'll be a special friend. But mostly, don't we want to be ourselves, by ourselves? I think we should stay all-girls," Elizabeth said emphatically.

"I don't want us to change," J.L. declared. "If we let boys join, we'd still have to go off somewhere to be alone with our girlfriends. We'd need two clubs."

"Who has time for that?"

Abby clapped her hands twice. "I call for a vote. Does anyone need more time?"

No one said anything, so Abby made it final. "A show of hands, then—all for keeping Zodiacs for girls only?"

Every hand in the room was raised.

"Hooray!" J.L. whooped. "It must be the right thing. It feels good."

"Uh-oh. Now comes the hard part." Mara swallowed. "Telling Danny the bad news."

"We'll do it together," Elizabeth said. "It won't be bad—he knows we still like him."

"Maybe we should call him up instead," Penny suggested wickedly. "All of us, one at a time, a phone call an hour—"

"Enough! Open the door and let them in."

Will hesitated at the doorway.

"Don't look scared, come in," J.L. called.

"Send Jen and Danny in," Cathy cried.

"They're not here."

"Not here?"

Cathy rushed to the door and peered outside. "What's going on?"

"You won't believe this." Will shrugged helplessly. "I think they went to play tennis." He looked totally bewildered—and to add to his surprise, Cathy grabbed him and hugged him.

"Tennis!" she yelled. "Tennis! Where? When did they leave?"

"A while ago, to the Academy courts. She challenged him."

"Don't worry. I'll tell them the news." She grabbed her

things and looped her arm through Will's, dragging him outside to his car.

"Please drive me to the Academy—I wouldn't miss this for the world."

"Okay. But what are we doing?"

"We're going to watch a tennis match—naturally. The final competition. Just leave it to Leo."

The tennis courts were nearly empty, so they easily spotted Jen and Danny. Danny was in the midst of a serve as Cathy and Will reached their court.

Will asked a boy retrieving tennis balls if he'd watched any of the match in the far court. "Who's winning?"

The boy picked up the ball he was chasing and gave Will a pitying look. "That girl is one of the worst players ever, and Burns can't get one point off her."

He moved off in disgust. Cathy pulled Will closer to the net.

Danny's serve wobbled and the ball flopped weakly into Jennifer's court, begging to be hit. Jennifer charged at it, swung, connected somehow, and scooped the ball over the net. Danny missed it.

"Your point," he called out.

Jennifer turned, saw Cathy, and waved. Then she made the worst toss Cathy had ever seen and missed her serve completely.

"I get it," Will said to Cathy. "Jennifer is trying not to win, and Danny is trying to lose."

"They're a perfect match," Cathy said, putting her arm around Will's waist.

"Did anyone actually score a point?" Will persisted.

"Will," Cathy said, pulling him closer, "there's only one score for this game—love all."

Cathy reached up and gave Will a kiss.

"What's that for?"

"Because I like you."

"I actually practiced for this match," Jennifer gasped, holding her sides.

"I'd hate to see you when you were bad," Cathy joked. "Before I forget, Jennifer—congratulations. You're the newest Zodiac."

Jennifer gasped in delight. "You're kidding." She hugged both Cathy and Will at once.

Danny came trotting up.

"Danny, I'm sorry, but the Zodiacs decided to stay all-girls." Cathy held out a hand. "No hard feelings."

Danny's smile faltered an instant. "No problem."

"You're not upset?" Jennifer looked at him.

"Who wants to be a boy in an all-girls club? Besides, I won't have time anymore. I'm going to be very busy."

Jennifer's smile clouded. "Oh? Doing what?"

Danny grinned. "Giving this girl tennis lessons." He put an arm around Jennifer's waist. "If she wants them," he added.

"She does."

Cathy had never seen Jennifer's dimples so deep and her smile so dazzling.

"Let's go to the diner," Danny said. "We'll celebrate—everything."

"No," Cathy said. "Let's go back to Abby's and be with all our friends."

Join in the fun when
THE ZODIAC CLUB™ meets
again in the following books:

THE STARS UNITE
(21106-3)
When summer doldrums hit, Abby Martin and her friends decide to change their fortunes by forming a club based on Abby's new passion, astrology. Little do they realize what the stars hold in store!

ARIES RISING
(21107-1)
What could be more perfect for Abby, an Aries, than a bike trip to Ram's Head Mountain at the spring equinox? Joining her science class on the trip means passing up a Zodiac Club weekend party, but Abby is ready for some adventure of her own...

TAURUS TROUBLE
(21109-8)
When Danny Burns scoops Cathy Rosen's story during their internship at the local newspaper, Cathy, a Leo, is roaring mad. Can she grab the bull by the horns and put the arrogant Taurus in his place?

LIBRA'S DILEMMA
(21108-X)
When Mara's boyfriend, Doug, is involved in a cheating scandal at Collingwood High, it's hard for Mara, the perfect Libra, to remain an impartial judge. Should she defend the guy she loves—or the principles she lives by?

$1.95 each

Join THE ZODIAC CLUB

You can be part of THE ZODIAC CLUB.
Share the fun and adventures
with the founding members.

Just fill out and return the coupon below
and you will receive:

★ **membership card** ★
★ **free personalized computerized horoscope** ★
★ **upcoming news of Zodiac Club titles** ★
★ **and more surprises** ★

_____ Yes! Enroll me in THE ZODIAC CLUB

Please send me my free personalized
computerized horoscope.

Name _____ Age _____
Address _____
City/State _____ Zip _____
Birthdate _____
       Day   Month   Year

                 A.M.
Time of birth _____ P.M. Place of birth _____
                                   City   State

Please enclose $1.50 to cover postage and handling.
Send check or money order — no cash or C.O.D.'s
please.

MAIL TO: Box Zodiac 3
              Pacer Books
              The Putnam Publishing Group
              51 Madison Avenue
              New York, NY 10010

...Because when you read about love, you're ready for it

We can't promise you a date on Saturday night, but we can promise you a good time when you curl up with a Two Hearts™ romance!

IN THE MIDDLE OF A RAINBOW by Barbara Girion
(21080-6)
When a chance meeting brings handsome Todd Marcus into her life, Corrie finds herself believing that dreams can come true!

LOVER'S GAMES by Barbara Cohen
(21081-4)
When Mandy attempts to fix up her cousin Lissa with Lissa's gorgeous new stepbrother, her matchmaking results in a comedy of errors!

ROADSIDE VALENTINE by C.S. Adler
(21146-2)
Seventeen-year-old Jamie is not about to let anyone stand in the way of his love for Louisa—not even Louisa's boyfriend!

VACATION FEVER! by Wendy Andrews
(21083-0)
Temperatures are on the rise and romance is in the air when Mia meets a handsome stranger on a family vacation!

$2.25 each

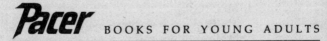